The Drawing Out Feelings Series

FACILITATORS GUIDE

FOR

LEADING GRIEF SUPPORT GROUPS

MARGE EATON HEEGAARD, MA, ATR, LICSW

With appreciation to the many professionals who have shared their knowledge, this work is dedicated to the young children who inspire and teach me... and to Roger for his caring and encouragement.

WOODLAND PRESS
99 Woodland Circle
Minneapolis, MN 55424
(612) 926-2665

PRINTED IN THE U.S.A.

TABLE OF CONTENTS

UNIT I.

Childhood Trauma and Crisis

There has been a great deal written in the past on the psychological effects of loss and separation during childhood on personality. Freud advanced the hypothesis in 1917 that much psychiatric illness is an expression of pathological mourning. More recently, John Bowlby's three volumes on attachment, separation, and loss, also link pathological conditions of later prevention of psychiatric disorders lie in learning more about the cause. Research has led him to believe that early loss can create many common clinical disorders including anxiety and phobia, depression and suicide, as well as disturbances of parenting and marriage.

PARENTS NEED TO KNOW HOW THEY CAN HELP CHILDREN DURING TIMES OF CRISIS

In times of crisis, explain the facts about the crisis in truthful calm words. Let the child be involved in age appropriate ways. Keep the family together if possible and mantain structure and as normal a routine as possible.

Assure children they are not the cause of the situation, nor could they have prevented it. Magical thinking gives children unrealistic powers.

Don't ignore children's fears...and don't over protect them. Listen to learn what their fears are and show an understanding. Help them to learn more about what they fear. Everyone fears the unknown.

Don't try to hide your own fears because children will be able to sense them. It is better to admit real fears and teach children safety measures for things like floods and earthquakes. Accept fears as healthy emotions and encourage children to share theirs without ridicule.

Ask children what they need to feel safe. The stronger they feel the easier it is for them to overcome fears. Let them play out their fears with toys to gain empowerment. Help them let go of unrealistic fears and develop coping skills for realistic fears. Children need courage to face hardships and wisdom to avoid unnecessary risks to face challenges and protect themselves.

Keep answering unending questions. Don't be afraid to say, "I don't know." Try to find books that provide answers.

If children are entering a new situation, let them bring something familiar to provide securty for the transition.

Parents need to let children know where they will be so they can reach them if needed. Children need to know they are loved and they need holding and comforting from their parents. They need at least 10 minutes a day of one to one time from a parent...and more if possible. It may mean doing something the child chooses to do, but most important is being available to listen and observe the child.

Change needs to be prepared for in advance and coping skills need to be developed at an early age for crisis events. Pets are very important to children because they make them feel needed and they are something they usually can count on being there for them. The loss of a pet is good time to teach coping skills for loss and change. Awareness and acceptance of feelings must be taught at an early age. Very young children can learn that feelings affect behavior and learn accepted forms of expression.

Children need to be assured they are loveable and will always be taken care of.

WHEN SOMEONE HAS A SERIOUS ILLNESS

Society is just beginning to recognize the effects of extended serious illness on a family. Chronic or terminal illness may create economic hardships, relocation and other changes, demands on adult time and emotional stresses that make a profound affect on children.

The effects can be similar to that of an alcoholic home where the focus is on the problems rather than the needs of the children who are often emotionally abandoned.

In both situations there is denial of the reality and severity of the problem. Both families often repress feelings and become isolated from social contacts. Children do not have two parents they can count on when one is sick and they often grow up with responsibilities beyond their years even if it is a child that is the one with the serious illness.

Feelings of insecurity and fear overwhelm and confuse children when they are developmentally too young to cope with them. They often feel shame for natural feelings of anger and resentment. They develop defenses and wear masks to hide difficult "inside" feelings.

Children often develop roles of creating or fixing problems, being unavailable or too perfect, being a clown to make an unhappy family feel good or or anything that works to get their own needs met. These roles often continue as a personality problem in adulthood. They can grow up to be overly responsible, lose healthy spontaneity and over react to change. There is often a lack of trust, a need to control and a fear of abandonment.

Group experience with others in a similar situation gives children the opportunity to move out of isolation and silence. They can learn to be more flexible and spontaneous if they are given the opportunity to develop trust and coping skills. Children need to learn basic facts about the illness to reduce fears from misconceptions and learn how to take care of themselves to reduce insecurities.

Information may be requested from national organizations to help them understand more about the illness, books can be checked out of school and local libraries, and hospitals are beginning to offer support groups for children when a family member has a serious illness.

This curriculum is designed to help children recognize, name and accept personal feelings and learn acceptable ways to express them. Children are encouraged to recognize personal strengths and increase self esteem. Children who are able to particpate will learn they are not alone in their struggle and identify and use available support systems. The workbook offers helpful suggestions to adults in supportive relationships as well as professionals. If a group of children is unavailable, the organized approach also works well with children on an individual basis.

WHEN SOMETHING TERRIBLE HAPPENS

Traumatic events in the lives of children leave them feeling frightened and insecure. Overwhelming feelings create confusion and defenses that often become unhealthy patterns of coping.

Floods, earthquakes, tornados and other violent acts of nature which terrify adults are even more frightening for children who have limited understanding. Physical or sexual abuse, rape, murder and other violent acts of human beings can be just as frightening and occur more frequently. Violent and mutilating deaths such as suicide or plane crashes and near death experiences can cause post traumatic stress.

Post traumatic stress occurs when an individual is exposed to an overwhelming event that results in helplessness in the face of intolerable danger, anxiety and instinctual arousal, and results in significant impairment of pyschological and adaptive functioning.

The symptoms of post traumatic stress lasting in excess of one month are: persistant and intrusive re-experiencing or recollections of the traumatic event, avoidance of stimuli associated with the event, numbing of general responsiveness, and increased arousal not present prior to event.

Drawing a traumatic event empowers a child and presents the opportunity to overcome feelings of helplessness and fear.

This curriculum offers group structure which is helpful for natural disasters when large numbers of children have been affected. School counselors and therapists can offer support in situations when groups are appropriate. Art therapy is helpful in assessing children for referral for individual therapy.

The guide and workbook also aids professionals when individual therapy is appropriate. It can be used with children as young as three when the therapist invites the child to tell him/her what to draw...and they work together on the pages. Very young children begin with meaningful scribbles and tell an important story about their picture. The pages provide direction for difficult situations.

Timing is important. Early phases of shock and denial must be respected and the child allowed to decide when and what to draw. Pages can be skipped because they are not relevant...or because they are still too painful. Most children, however find it e easier to draw a traumatic experience than to talk about it and nightmares often stop after drawing them. It is never to early to begin to understand feelings.

Traumatic Bereavement

Eth, S. and Pynoos, R., Interaction of trauma and grief in childhood in Eth, S. and Pynoos, R. (eds.), <u>Post-traumatic Stress Disorder in Children</u>, Washington, D. C., American Psychiatric Press, 1985, p. 169 - 186.

Furman, E. When is the death of a parent traumatic? Psychoanalytic Study of the Child, Vol. 41, 186, p. 191 - 209.

Pynoos, R. and Eth, S. Witness to violence: the child interview. Journal of the American Academy of Child Psychiatry, 25, 3:306 - 319, 1986.

Pynoos, R., Nader, K., et al, Grief reactions in school age children following a sniper attack at the school. Israeli Journal of Psychiatry and Related Sciences. Vol. 24, nos 1-2, 53 - 63, 1987. *

Developmental Characteristics

COGNITIVE	SOCIAL	SELF	VALUES	ARTISTIC

5-7 YEARS

COGNITIVE	SOCIAL	SELF	VALUES	ARTISTIC
° differentiates clearly between fantasy and reality ° attention span by age 7 shows dramatic lengthening - has ability to shift attention ° concepts are largely functional ° can order objects on dimensions of size and quantity ° memory good for concrete sequences (numbers) ° is able to give more thought to judgments and decisions	° beginnings of empathy; sees others point of view ° two or three best friends ° play groups are small and of short duration ° quarrels frequent, but short ° beginning of conformity with peers (dress, language) ° peers become increasingly important ° beginning of sex cleavage; less boy-girl interaction	° clarifies differences between adult and ° achieves independence in physical self care ° gaining practical knowledge necessary for everyday living ° exploration is more goal directed ° learning to forego immediate reward for delayed gratification	° sense of duty and accomplishment ° developing consciousness · is in evidence; resulting from behavior may be rigid and expressed in extremes ° beginning to accept there are rules, but does not understand the principles behind them	Period of greatest qualitative differences between sequences Images reflect movement from a single aspect of an object or form to pictorial sequencing Several objects may be related in one drawing Pictorial images begin to tell stories

8-10 YEARS

COGNITIVE	SOCIAL	SELF	VALUES	ARTISTIC
° capable of prolonged interest ° see similarities ° can apply logical thought to practical situations ° beginning to understand relationship of cause and effect ° understands concept of money ° understands concept of time; has ability to plan ahead	° intensification of peer group influence ° cliques of the same sex ° both boys and girls interested in hobbies ° competition more common, with considerable boasting ° overly concerned with peer imposed rules ° antagonism between boys and girls leads to frequent quarrels ° extreme energy expenditure in physical game playing	° conforms to sex role ° achieving personal independence ° aware of importance of belonging ° self-sufficient, can do things independently inside and outside the home	° testing and questioning attitudes, values, belief systems; may result in conflict ° adult role models give strong clues about acceptable behaviors ° understands the reason for rules and behaves according to them ° beginning to make value judgments about own behavior, set standards for self, accept responsibility for behavior	Period of realistic representation of familiar objects Relationships are drawn in more orderly fashion Elevated base lines and ground lines appear Human figures move from static to action related representational images More frontal and profile views of people and objects appear Houses and people take on a more proportional relationship

11-13 YEARS

COGNITIVE	SOCIAL	SELF	VALUES	ARTISTIC
° transition from concrete to abstract thinking; uses abstract words ° emergence of independent critical thinking ° can apply logic to solve problems; thinks inductively ° can solve problems by considering alternatives	° peers become source of behavior standards and models ° conforms to rules assigned by group ° team games popular ° crushes and hero worship are common for same and opposite sex ° boisterous behavior common ° self-consciousness creates anxiety about behavior ° faced with decisions regarding alcohol and drug use	° achieves a masculine or feminine social role ° learning one's role in heterosexual relationships ° seeking self-identity sometimes includes rebellion ° self-concept is influenced by bodily changes	° asserting and developing own value system although peer influence is strong ° understands ethical abstractions (example: justice, honesty) ° beginning to be aware of and discuss social issues	

Minnesota Department of Education, June 1988.

The mental health needs of children

Mental health is just as important to children, parents and families as physical health. Sometimes a child's behavior may make a parent wonder if something is wrong with their child's mental health. When should parents seek mental health services for their children and themselves?

It can be confusing to sort out the differences between normal child behavior, temporary difficulties or "phases," and signs of major emotional or mental health problems.

There are some signs that warn parents and children that they may need professional advice or help. When these signs continue or return over many weeks and disrupt family life, the child's behavior with peers or at school, parents and children can benefit from seeking professional help.

Help for parents

A cornerstone of family health is the willingness to deal with and talk about problems or stress with someone who can help. The first step is to share your concerns with a level-headed, trustworthy and well-informed helper. Talking things out relieves tension and helps people to see situations in a clearer light and to see what might be done about them. Parent education, parent support and parent counseling programs can help parents who often feel unprepared or uncertain about being a parent. Special programs may provide valuable aids to parents in particularly stressful situations, for example, single parents, step-parents, adoptive parents, foster parents or parents of children with special needs. Getting help to improve their confidence, skill and understanding about being a parent are some of the most helpful thing parents can do for their child.

Finding mental health services for children

Early identification and treatment of mental health problems can improve children's well-being and can help prevent more serious difficulties in later life. Consultation with a child development specialist at school, with a doctor, or at a child and family mental health service, can help pinpoint a potential problem and develop a plan of action. This plan could include a program of counseling or therapy for the child, the parent(s), or the family together.

Warning signs

Symptoms that point to the need for child and/or family mental health services may include:

Emotional signs

* unreasonable or extreme fears

* anxiety, worry, tension, or nervousness that may be vague or may be associated with particular situations such as being separated from the family, speaking or performing in public, taking tests or entering strange situations

* depressed mood, indicated by continual sadness, low self-esteem, boredom or lack of interest; loss of energy, optimism or enthusiasm; a sense of hopelessness and/or preoccupation with morbid ideas

* lack of self-confidence, self-esteem or self-worth, poor self-concept, feelings of inadequacy, inferiority or self-doubt

Behavioral signs

* marked changes from usual patterns of behavior (quiet person becomes wild, or active person becomes withdrawn)

* continual violations of major rules and of the rights of others

* risk-taking, recklessness or accident-proneness

* isolated, withdrawn, overly-inhibited behavior

* escapist behaviors, including running away

* chronic defiance or lack of response to rules, routines and discipline

* disturbances in bodily regulation and self-care, including disturbances of eating and weight regulation, disturbances of sleep, problems with bowel or bladder control and other routines

* experimentation or use of mood-altering chemicals or drugs

continued on opposite side

Social-interactional signs

- problems relating to peers, difficulty making or keeping friends, isolation or loneliness

- problems in relating to adults as authority figures or in establishing trusting, satisfying relationships with adult caretakers

- excessive conflict with peers, brothers and sisters, parents and/or other adults

- family stress and relationship difficulties involving parent-child interaction; changes in families due to separation, loss, divorce, economic problems; parenting problems or adjustments relating to adoption or to placement away from the parental home

School-related difficulties

- delays in readiness for school learning, due to immaturity in physical development, large and small muscle coordination; delays in ability to learn, and social/emotional immaturity

- difficulty in establishing the motivation and attitudes needed to shift to the achievement and "work" expectations of school

- problems with attention, concentration or organization for school tasks

- problems with learning style or specific skills that may indicate learning disorders or disability

- excessive anxiety about school performance, perfectionism or inability to tolerate or to risk failure

- fearfulness or negative attitudes about school, leading to excessive absence, truancy, refusal or avoidance of attending school

- social, emotional or behavioral interference with comfortable adjustment to school

Emotional symptoms related to physical health

- difficulty in adjusting to the impact of physical illness, injury handicap or chronic disease that may show up as emotional, behavioral, interactional or school-related difficulties

- symptoms and complaints like chronic fatigue and the vague or specific sense of "not feeling well" without identified physical or medical cause

- stress that originates in the child's emotional, social, family or school life may contribute to the development of stress-related symptoms such as recurrent headaches, stomachaches, and other physical problems; or it may contribute to or complicate a physical illness

Child mental health emergencies

Fortunately, it is unusual for preadolescent children to develop symptoms that indicate a sudden and severe mental health crisis. There are, however, a few situations where immediate protection and attention to diagnosis and treating problems is called for. If your child shows these signs, seek emergency service immediately through a health care clinic, family physician, hotline, or local crisis or emergency care center. These situations include:

- threats, attempts or persistent thoughts about self-injury or suicide

- dangerous, intense, destructive, or violent behaviors, including fire-setting or assault

- acute agitation, distress or inconsolable emotional pain

- severe withdrawal, isolation and inability to carry on daily routines, including getting to school.

Minneapolis Children's Medical Center

Minneapolis Children's Medical Center offers a full range of specialized services for children, from infants to adolescents, and their families. MCMC's philosophy of care is child- and family-oriented and focuses on emotional as well as physical well-being. Families may request help for their children or themselves, or can be referred to programs by helping professionals. To learn more about the mental health services of Minneapolis Children's Medical Center, contact:

Intake coordinator
Minneapolis Children's Medical Center
2525 Chicago Avenue So.
Minneapolis, MN 55404
612/863-6888

This information was prepared by Susan E. Erbaugh, PhD., Licensed Consulting Psychologist and director of mental health service, Minneapolis Children's Medical Center.

December 1989

WHEN A FAMILY IS IN STRESS DUE TO ILLNESS, DIVORCE, DEATH OR OTHER SIGNIFICANT CHANGE, CHILDREN SENSE THE STRESS OF OTHERS AND FEEL HELPLESS AND INSECURE. THIS OFTEN LEADS TO HYPERACTIVITY, BEHAVIORAL AND ATTITUDINAL PROBLEMS WHICH CAN BE REDUCED BY PROVIDING MORE STRUCTURE IN THEIR LIVES.

Providing Structure to Reduce Stress

I.   BE CONSISTENT

    A. Avoid threats and exaggerated statements that you are unable to follow through.

    B. Parental figures need to agree on expectations and rules and be supportive to each other.

    C. Don't allow children to manipulate you into changing your mind.

    D. Establish routine times for bedtime, meals, and homework.

    E. Follow up to see if child did what was requested.

II. SET RULES

    A. Tell children what your rules or expectations are.

    B. Tell them what will happen if they follow rules, and what will happen if they don't...and allow them to be responsible for their decision.

    C. State rules and consequences one at a time.

    D. Be specific...set up consequences for each behavior.

III. SET CONSEQUENCES FOR BEHAVIOR

TYPES OF CONSEQUENCES

I.   IGNORING...OR NO CONSEQUENCE

This is a powerful method of discipline, but not often used effectively by parents. Generally, this consequence should be tried first. If it doesn't work, try positive or negative consequence.

    A. Do not ignore behavior that is task oriented, disrupts activities of others, or may lead to injury to self or damage to property.

    B. Do use if the behavior is manipulative, designed to upset the parent, or will lead to a power struggle. (temper tantrums, whining, pouting, etc.)

    C. Withdraw all attention...or withdraw emotional attention and deal only with behavior.

    D. To be effective, this discipline must be consistent, and child must be truly ignored verbally and non-verbally.

TWENTY MEMOS FROM YOUR CHILD

1. Don't spoil me. I know quite well that I ought not to have all I ask for—I'm only testing you.

2. Don't be afraid to be firm with me. I prefer it; it makes me feel secure.

3. Don't let me form bad habits. I have to rely on you to detect them in the early stages.

4. Don't make me feel smaller than I am. It only makes me behave stupidly "big."

5. Don't correct me in front of people if you can help it. I'll take much more notice if you talk quietly with me in private.

6. Don't make me feel that my mistakes are sins. It upsets my sense of values.

7. Don't protect me from consequences. I need to learn the painful way sometimes.

8. Don't be too upset when I say "I hate you." Sometimes it isn't you I hate but your power to thwart me.

9. Don't take too much notice of my small ailments. Sometimes they get me the attention I need.

10. Don't nag. If you do, I shall have to protect myself by appearing deaf.

11. Don't forget that I cannot explain myself as well as I should like. That is why I am not always accurate.

12. Don't put me off when I ask questions. If you do, you will find that I stop asking and seek my information elsewhere.

13. Don't be inconsistent. That completely confuses me and makes me lose faith in you.

14. Don't tell me my fears are silly. They are terribly real and you can do much to reassure me if you try to understand.

15. Don't ever suggest that you are perfect or infallible. It gives me too great a shock when I discover that you are neither.

16. Don't ever think that it is beneath your dignity to apologize to me. An honest apology makes me feel surprisingly warm toward you.

17. Don't forget I love experimenting. I couldn't get along without it, so please put up with it.

18. Don't forget how quickly I am growing up. It must be very difficult for you to keep pace with me, but please try.

19. Don't forget that I don't thrive without lots of love and understanding, but I don't need to tell you, do I?

20. Please keep yourself fit and healthy. I need you.

(Author unknown)

Increasing Children's Self Esteem

People who have positive self esteem know they are loveable and capable and they care about themselves and others. They look and feel good and are effective and productive. Jean Illsey Clark in "SELF ESTEEM: A FAMILY AFFAIR" believes we build our brand of self-esteem from four ingredients: fate, the positive things life offers, the negative things life offers, and our own decision about how to respond to these ingredients. A child's self-esteem is often damaged when fate takes a loved one by death, and the child feels abandoned. It does not have to be a permanent negative effect, and it is important to find opportunities to strengthen self-esteem. Children, ages 6-12, need to be able to explore and understand rules. They need to be able to try out their values and ways of doing things to get their own needs met. They need to be able to incorporate their own rules into their heads solidly enough to enable them to begin to take care of themselves. They need to be able to disagree with others and find out they won't go away.

Adults can help children build self-esteem by being gentle, supportive, and caring. They need to allow children to get their needs met. Adults can offer to help and give permission to succeed and affirm them. Adults also need to be able to set limits, protect, and teach ethics and ways to succeed. Children need to learn to be able to trust their feelings, and to learn that they do not have to suffer to get what they need.

Children grieve the loss of the family unit when a family changes. They are confused about feelings. They often act angry when they are actually feeling sad or frightened. A loss experienced by a friend, re-marriage of a parent, anniversary of a death or additional losses may precipitate another cycle of grief and a decline in self esteem.

Extended separation from a parent for any reason can shake the foundation of trust in young children. It creates feelings of powerlessness and shame which makes self control more difficult. When parents are unavailable children often develop negative ways to get attention. They need to learn new ways of getting positive attention. Age appropriate chores and responsibilities can be rewarded with genuine praise, hugs, allowances and undivided attention.

Older siblings often resent and put down younger children. Children need to learn healthy self talk to counter this. All children need to feel more powerful to counter feelings of helplessness. Instead of picking on someone smaller to feel strong, they can HELP someone smaller and feel helpful. They need invitations to help at home and at school. They like to do things that are still a bit difficult.

Children act out helplessness by trying to control their own or other's lives. Bossiness, challenging rules, fighting, and beligerent behavior becomes frequent. They need to learn how to make choices and decisions in some areas of their life. Rules can be discussed and verbal disagreement allowed for consideration.

Solving family problems together is helpful. The problem needs to be identified and discussed. All kinds of solutions can be suggested and listed on paper. Discuss and eliminate poor solutions. Discuss and choose better ones to try. Fair and loving authority will be respected. Structure and rules make them feel loved and secure.

Affirmations for Growth

At each period or stage of growth in children's lives there are certain tasks they need to master and certain decisions they need to make if they are to grow into loving, capable, responsible adults.

Parents can help children master these tasks by providing safe, structured, stimulating environments and experiences. Parents can encourage their children to make appropriate decisions by challenging inappropriate behavior and by giving their children affirmations.

What are affirmations? Affirmations are all the things we do or say that imply that children are lovable and capable. We affirm children with our words and our actions, our body language, our facial expressions, and our tone of voice.

Here are some special affirming messages that will help children in this stage of growth (ages six through twelve), when they are developing their own structures, competence, and values, and are learning about the relevance of rules.

Affirmations for Structure

- You can think before you say yes or no and learn from your mistakes.
- You can trust your intuition to help you decide what to do.
- You can find a way of doing things that works for you.

- You can learn the rules that help you live with others.
- You can learn when and how to disagree.
- You can think for yourself and get help instead of staying in distress.
- I love you even when we differ; I love growing with you.

You give these affirmations by the way you interact with your children, challenge their thinking, and encourage them to test values, examine rules, acquire information and skills, and experience consequences.

In addition to all the things you do, you can *say* these affirmations directly in supportive, loving ways.

Belief in these affirmations helps children achieve independence and encourages them to develop strong, internal self-responsibility. The affirmations are powerful antidotes to peer pressure. Giving them may take effort, especially on days when the children are hassling you and pushing the limits to find out what rules are firm and important and what happens when rules are broken.

Of course, you have to believe these messages yourself, or they become confusing or crazy double messages. If you don't understand or believe an affirmation, don't give that one until you do believe it.

Once human beings have entered each developmental stage, they need to receive the affirmations from that stage for the rest of their lives, so children continue to need the affirmations from earlier stages.

From: HELP! FOR PARENTS OF CHILDREN 6-12 YEARS, Clarke, Gradous, Sittko and Ternand   Harper & Row, San Franciso 1986

Art Therapy for Coping with Change

Art therapy is appropriate to every age and cultural background. There are two basic theories of art therapy. Margaret Naumberg in the 1930's stressed the importance of working out unconscious material through the portrayal of symbols. Relationships, concepts of self, and other concepts may be revealed this way. In the 1950's Edith Kramer developed a second theory which stresses the process of creative activity as a natural and compelling activity which builds self identity. Both are nonverbal communication which encourage integration of the person.

Creativity is the conversion of symbolic imagery and fantasy into something tangible such as a painting, poem, or musical composition in a form that can be shared with others. Converting unconscious fantasy into a work of art brings with it greater self awareness, ego strength, and self esteem. Releasing feelings through creativity is a unique function of art therapy.

Creating art is an appropriate outlet for expressing fears of death and feelings of grief that children are neither able to understand or express. Children can draw death as the "cavemen" did by drawing a feared animal or a fearful event to defeat it, thus overcoming their fears. Inappropriate impulses can be channeled into positive experiences.

Art provides a method for expressing repressed feelings, and becomes a tool for overcoming defenses, understanding, consolidating earlier losses, and increasing cognitive understanding of the present while encouraging feelings of independence and maturation. Art therapy attempts to utilize cognitive and effective levels of relating through concrete/spacial art work and linear/verbal therapy. It also offers opportunities for transference.

Bereavement art seems to follow three distinct natural stages and are similar to the process of grief. The first is the degree of awareness or denial of the conflict creating stress. The second is expressing the feeling and suffering of mourning. The last stage is seen as resolution when death is seen as part of life. Some art work seems to be directly influenced by the need to express unconscious feelings about death. They may be expressed either in a traditional style using conventional subject to express emotions, or the emotions may be expressed in the form of archaic symbols and color. Either style may take a massive or linear style and the process of grief is revealed as the style changes.

Meaningful art therapy needs to occur in a secure situation where needs will be supported by the empathy, acceptance, active listening and authenticity of a caring art therapist, and preferably one who understands the grief process from personal experience.

Children need to explore the abstract realm of feelings, to accept and own all feelings. They also need to learn to identify problem feelings and defensive reactions to them. Children seem to be able to learn these concepts at an early age, and the need to deny overwhelming emotions is reduced it there is some understanding. As defense reactions, children tend to become: silent, overly responsible for others, overly achieving, angry, entertaining and distracting, or dependent on using outside things to forget. Children seem able to recognize these defensive ways of reacting to uncomfortable feelings like sadness, fear, and anger.

In art or play, the child may do the impossible. He may fulfill symbolically both positive wishes and negative impulses without fear of real consequences. He can gain symbolic access to and relive past traumas and can rehearse and practice for the future. It is Judith Rubin's conviction that children cannot learn to control and organize if the structure does not ultimately come from within. An adult offering art must provide a framework which does not impose controls and make the child dependent on, but a structure which allows the child to be free to think and fantasize. A child needs a safe and supportive network in which he/she can freely struggle to order and control.

Encouraging children to clarify and verbalize ideas and feelings without imposing or intruding one's own projections is challenging, but necessary. Questions such as "Can you tell me something about this picture?" or "Who might the suns, flowers, etc. be if they were people?" are helpful.

Symbolic Messages in Children's Art

"Universal symbols" have some degree of validity and it is important to consider these meanings as possibilities, but it is more important to rely heavily on what is observed and what makes sense in the context of the actual encounter with a child in art. Art therapists are trained at graduate level to use art to assess an individual's current functioning as well as mental and cognitive maturity. They are trained in symbolic language and other forms of nonverbal communication to help children and adults integrate self awareness and self expression within a therapeutic relationship. Clinical psychologists and other professionals also use drawings for assessment purposes.

I do not recommend the untrained person to search for hidden meanings in children's art. I do believe anyone can consider art as communication, and respond to an obvious pictoral message the same as they would respond to the same message in words. Children may express fears and anger that they are unable to express verbally. Drawings of the human figure can be considered a reflection of the individual's emotional conflicts and attitudes. Assessment is made on the overall quality of the drawing, specific features and ommisssions of details. Observations of behavior while drawing is also important. Choice of color, or lack of color, is significant. Excessive use of red is often associated with anger, and continued use of very dark colors suggest depression. Individual color preferences vary greatly, and all art work must be considered only as clues for further assessment.

The art work of children who have experienced something very traumatic will often show emotional regression. Figures are often very small and there will be poor figure integration. The drawing is often highly constricted. There are few details and it is below chronological drawing ability. There is often fixation on the traumatic event and will be drawn without being asked for.

The constricted focus is on one or more specific symbols. There is not much interest in background detail or integration. There is usually a lack of color and other depression indicators such as a sad sun or clouds are included.

Somatic indicators of boxed in monsters, stomach area emphasis, armless or legless people indicating powerlessness are common. There are a variety of expressions of anger and anxiety. Drawing circles or boxes around people or things, erasures, crossing out parts, floating ungrounded figures are often drawn. Rainbows and butterflies may be drawn as more hopeful signs...sometimes much later.

Fears, guilt, shame and anxiety are more apparent in emotional crisis. Art often expresses feelings of helplessness and unsolveable problems. Denial, repression and alienation can be the beginning of behavioral problems and maladaptation.

Art therapy crisis resolution can utilize present adaptive skill while it helps develop socially acceptable problem solving skills. The anger, guilt and grief that is expressed on paper must be accepted to discourage repression. The event can be explored and difficult emotions expressed more easily on paper than verbally. Perceptions can be clarified.

Avoidance of reality indicates denial. Some pages in the workbooks in the "DRAWING OUT FEELING SERIES" may be skipped or something unrelated will be drawn. A dead person may be included with the living or a sick person may be drawn as healthy and strong. Divorced parents may be drawn as living together...instead of broken hearts which are seen often with children of divorced parents.

The workbooks begin with drawing tasks related to life changes partly as an introduction to change, and also for an indication of drawing interest and ability before emotional pages.

Crayons are suggested because they allow for more variety of pressure than markers. Soft lines and pictures indicate insecurity. Strong bold sharp lines indicate aggressive feelings. Colored pencils can be available for older children who want to add more detail. Older children may also choose to use more words, but drawings represent more true feelings.

The "Scribble In" activities in the group sessions of this guide offer an opportunity to relax or energize children after a day in the classroom. "Scribble Out" offers a release of energy and feelings after an emotional time in group. Both activities are enjoyed by children and encourage expression of feelings

It is normal for children who have experienced loss and change or crisis to have these indicators in their art. Some intervention is always helpful. Art is a healthy intervention for children who express themselves with pictures more easily than in words.

Coalition News

Monthly newsletter of the MN Coalition
for Death Education and Support, Inc.
Vol. 13, No. 10
October, 1990

This months lead article contributor is board
member **Marge Heegaard**. Marge is an art
therapist and LICSW.

Art As Therapy With The Grieving

Art Therapy and other creative humanistic strategies
are becoming popular methods for working with life-
threatened patients and bereaved family members.
Kubler-Ross and the Simontons have demonstrated
the effectiveness of non-verbal communication techniques such as visualization and drawing.

Art enables the elderly and the terminally ill to face
repressed feelings about death. I have used art in
workshops to relate more humanely with patients.
Similar techniques used with teachers have helped
them to recognize the impact loss has on children. I
also use art therapy with grieving adults to help them
develop self awareness and recognize emotional
conflicts and encourage integration.

The act of drawing stimulates repressed memories of
the unconscious and brings them into awareness for
healing. Art can be used to facilitate early loss recall
and identify patterns of reaction to loss developed in
childhood and often repeated with current significant
loss. Unhealthy patterns can be changed when identified.

Looking back at the pain of childhood loss with the
eyes of an adult invites a new and more understanding perspective. .Current trauma that explodes in the
mind can be captured and controlled on a sheet of
paper. Adults often feel threatened by art materials
so I combine art with traditional grief therapy.

Children respond eagerly to bereavement art therapy
out of the need to express conscious and unconscious feelings of grief and death fears. Children
have a natural tendency to repress painful feelings
but find covert expression in art materials.

Crayons are more effective than markers to express a
wide range of feelings because they respond more to
pressure. Clay is an effective release for anger. The
"sand tray" is a favorite choice for most children in
individual grief therapy. Choosing from a wide
variety of miniatures they create a fantasy they can
control. They often create imaginary battles of good
and evil, releasing feelings of rage and injustice in
ways that are accepted and non-destructive. They
are able to act out and overcome feelings of fear,
anger and helplessness.

Art therapy often begins with a scribble drawing and
expressing feelings with color, lines and shapes.
Children and adults both need to recognize feelings
as something they feel in their bodies. They quickly
learn the places they "stuff" difficult feelings are often
the same places they develop pains. Stomach aches,
headaches and disturbing nightmares often cease
after art therapy.

Bereavement art therapy seems to follow three natural stages which correspond with the grief process.
The first is the degree of awareness of denial of
reality. The second is the expression of the feelings
and suffering of mourning. The last is seen as resolution when death is portrayed as part of life.

My book, *When Someone Very Special Dies*, is an
organized approach for using art with bereaved
children individually or in groups to help them
express thoughts and feelings while gaining needed
educational concepts. My most recent book, *Coping
With Death*, for grades 3-6, has just been published
by Lerner Publications.

Registered art therapists (ATR) are trained to meet
professional requirements set by the American Art
Therapy Association. Persons with undergraduate
degrees in art, art therapy, psychology or human
services are eligible to pursue graduate training in art
therapy.

*THE AMERICAN ART THERAPY ASSOCIATION
1202 Allanson Road
Mundelein, Il. 60060
(708) 949-6064*

MARGE HEEGAARD, ATR, LICSW
Grief Counseling · Art Therapy

99 Woodland Circle
Edina, Minnesota 55424
(612) 926-2665

UNIT II.

Facilitating Children's Support Groups

Not everyone is comfortable facilitating grief support groups because of the reminders of past losses and separation issues, fears of future losses, and personal mortality. It is important to become aware of personal death anxiety.

If a facilitator has experienced and resolved personal grief issues, it is possible to have gained compassion that is beneficial for working with others. Unresolved issues and apprehension over feared losses can get in the way of effective support for others. Working with the bereaved can make one anxious about their own mortality until they come to terms with this reality. (Worden 1982)

Children are especially able to sense an adult's comfort level when talking about death. I have found it is very important to devote considerable time during my facilitator training workshops to help participants explore their own history of losses. Sharing feelings, behaviors and support remembered as a child helps adults recognize how differently children grieve. It is also an opportunity to recognize any unresolved issues and areas of conflict. It can be a very healing process to look back at early childhood losses with the more mature eyes and understanding of an adult.

Deep rooted psychological disturbances are often related to awareness of one's personal death creating feelings of helplessness and vulnerability. This can create: (1) fear and anxiety leading to neurotic behavior (2) futility and alienation leading to existential depression or (3) frustration and anger leading to homicidal aggression. (Worden 1976)

People often use withdrawal, avoidance distraction, fatalistic acceptance, blaming self or others to reduce vulnerability and helplessness which accompanies the dread of death. None are effective. Worden suggest more effective ways of coping are:

1. Seek additional information about the problem.
2. Confront the problem and take action to resolve it.
3. Redefine the problem to see something favorable about it.
4. Share your concerns about the problem with other people.

This is basic strategy for coping with fears, and grief support groups for both children and adults are opportunities to use these strategies. Breaking fear from fears of death gives one true freedom to live and enjoy life.

FACILITATOR ROLES

TEACH BASIC CONCEPTS
HELP CHILDREN RECOGNIZE, ACCEPT, AND EXPRESS FEELINGS
PROVIDE OPPORTUNITIES FOR RISKS & PROBLEM SOLVING
ENCOURAGE OPEN COMMUNICATION & OPPORTUNITIES TO LEARN FROM EACH OTHER
GIVE SUPPORT & ENCOURAGEMENT
DISCOVER UNHEALTHY MISCONCEPTIONS

Helping Adults Understand Loss and Change

Life indicates growing and growth involves change. Change always creates loss. The loss may be tangible and easy to recognize or it may be symbolic and more difficult to identify. GRIEF is the normal reaction to loss and is part of existence.

Individuals will all grieve differently depending on the nature of the loss and relationship involved, timeliness and cause of the loss, previous losses and ability to cope, and support system available.

Significant loss can cause symptoms that are often mistaken for pathology. Preoccupation, guilt, hostile reactions, bodily distress and inability to function is normal grief behavior. Society expects people to grieve about two weeks instead of the more likely two years for the loss of a spouse by death...or one year for every 5 years of marriage that ends in divorce.

Sadness, Anger, guilt, self reproach, anxiety, loneliness, fatigue, helplessness, shock, yearning as well as relief are all normal feelings of grief. Disbelief, hallucinations, sense of presence and confusion of thoughts are all common.

Sleep and appetite disturbances, social withdrawal, dreams, avoidance, crying, clinging, inability to concentrate or overactivity are behaviors associated with normal grief reactions.

In 1969, Kubler-Ross outlined 5 stages of grief. Since most of her work was with the dying, these stages are most often used to understand a person's reaction to a terminal illness or death after a chronic illness or a troubled marriage and other anticipated losses.

1. DENIAL & ISOLATION
2. BARGAINING
3. ANGER
4. DEPRESSION
5. ACCEPTANCE

Originally presented by Bowlby in 1969 and modified by Parkes in 1974 and currently most often referred to as the response to all kinds of significant loss are four phases.

1. SHOCK OR PROTEST
2. YEARNING AND SEARCHING
3. DISORGANIZATION AND DESPAIR
4. REORGANIZATION

This seems to suggest that grief occurs in some neat order, which is not true. Phases may overlap, and they return. The intensity of grief may seem the same but the periods of grief will be shorter and the time between increases.

Time alone does not heal. Worden believes the four basic tasks of grief are:

1. TO ACCEPT THE REALITY OF THE LOSS
2. TO EXPERIENCE THE FEELINGS OF GRIEF
3. TO ADJUST TO LIVING WITHOUT THE ONE LOST
4. TO INVEST ENERGY IN NEW RELATIONSHIPS

Parke's and Weiss believe that three tasks need to take place for recovery from grief:

1. INTELLECTUAL RECOGNITION AND EXPLANATION OF THE LOSS
2. EMOTIONAL ACCEPTANCE OF THE LOSS
3. ASSUMPTION OF A NEW IDENTITY

Basic Group Structure

This structure is flexible to fit into 1 hour sessions, or expand to 1 1/2 hour sessions. Groups may need to fit into 50-60 minute school periods or expand to coordinate with adult groups meeting at a similar time in hospitals and churches.

1 1/2 hours is ideal when available. When time, space, budget, and resources are limited, it is possible to expand this basic structure without adding the optional activities. This is also suggested when there is a wide range of ages. Six and twelve year olds can be more comfortable drawing together than playing some of the same games and exercises.

Small groups require less time for discussion than larger groups. Younger children may need more movement exercises.

5 minutes	**BEGINNING**	Snack "SCRIBBLE IN"
10 minute (optional)		WELCOMING ACTIVITY
40-50 minute	**CONTENT**	REVIEW (weeks 2-6, last week, we...) INTRODUCTION (today, we will...) DRAW SHARE
10 minute (optional)		ACTIVITY EXERCISE
5 minute	**ENDING**	SUMMARY (today, we did...) NEXT WEEK PREP (next week, we'll...) SCRIBBLE OUT CREATIVE GOODBYE

I BEGINNING

SNACK: Children like treats, and adult can sign up to bring something for the group on a certain day. It should be simple, and the child that brings it can serve it. They really like to do this, and it is more important than it may seem. Keep books away until finished.

I begin 4:30 sessions with a snack, and would also suggest evening meeting to begin this way. It combines well with the "Scribble In", but others may choose to have the break mid-way.

RULES

THIS IS A PLACE WHERE CHILDREN CAN TALK ABOUT **CHANGE** AND LEARN TO COPE WITH FEELINGS OF GRIEF. IT IS A PLACE TO SHARE REAL FEELINGS AND LEARN FROM EACH OTHER. THERE ARE JUST A FEW RULES.

TREAT EACH OTHER WITH RESPECT (even your siblings!)
THERE ARE TIMES TO BE QUIET AND LISTEN.
MOST TIMES ARE FOR TALKING AND SHARING CONCERNS
IT'S O.K. TO CRY...AND O.K. TO LAUGH
WHAT IS SAID IN GROUPS STAYS IN GROUP. (CONFIDENTIAL.)

SCRIBBLE IN: This is a gathering time - something to do until
everyone is together. This helps break typical
school "confining" art practices where art is used
to teach following directions, etc. Stress that
art in this group is different; no rules, O.K. to
be messy, fix mistakes as best you can, color
<u>outside</u> the lines if you want, experiment!

Have plenty of newsprint available...it is easier
to learn to "waste."

CHECK IN: Choose one ritual to use as a check in...a
symbollic expression for the answer to "How are
you?" It can be a simple face,

Or the letter "I" drawn to show how you feel...

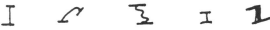

Or a pot (Virginia Satir?)

Or anything the group might choose to use.
Children like rituals, and they need some expected
rituals and structure to feel safe and secure in a
world they have lost so much so suddenly.

Or specific suggestions will be included in most
of the sessions to relate to the objectives.

GATHERING:

MUSIC: "WON'T YOU BE MY FRIEND?"
       Educational Activities

       "GETTING TO KNOW MYSELF"
       Hap Palmer

MOVEMENT: "LET'S SING AND PLAY"
          Bob Schneider   Golden Tape & book

BOOKS & FILMS: see bibliography

ACTIVITIES: several listed in some sessions

VISUALIZATIONS: create appropriately for each
                session.

Be careful to choose age appropriate activities that are not too difficult for the youngest, but not too "babyish" for the oldest. Choose activites you enjoy yourself. They need to be chosen to help understand and express feelings, build self esteem, increase or decrease energy levels and build relationship skills.

II CONTENT

LAST WEEK: After the first session, begin each session with a very BRIEF statement or two about what was done the week before. It is a chance to emphasize important concepts if there is time.

TODAY: Children want to know what they will be doing each day. Next, a book may be read to trigger thoughts and feelings they may have. Books are suggested in the book, and are all quite short for this purpose. Save discussions for later.

DRAW: Read the sentence at the top of the page they are going to draw. This is often enough. Children are used to being given more directions at school, and will often ask for more specifics. Simply reply, "This is your story, and you can do it any way you choose", or "how would you like to do it?"

It is not a perfect story...and doesn't have to be a perfect book!

Children past the 3rd grade often want more detail in their pictures, and may prefer to use pencils or narrow markers to crayons. I believe crayons are more expressive, and detailed drawing takes too much time for work of this nature.

Try not to compliment the children on their drawing ability. (You wouldn't say "You talk well!") Keep the emphasis on content, thoughts and feelings.

Drawing time is best kept non-verbal. Save discussions for later.

FEELINGS

EVERYBODY FEELS SOMETHING ALL OF THE TIME
SOMETIMES PEOPLE HAVE MIXED FEELINGS
ALL FEELINGS ARE O.K.   SOME ARE MORE DIFFICULT
FEELINGS NEED TO BE EXPRESSED
WE ARE RESPONSIBLE FOR OUR OWN FEELINGS
WE CANNOT CHANGE OTHER PEOPLE'S FEELINGS

SHARE: Ask "Who would like to tell us about their picture?" Listen, accept, and encourage additional information by saying, "Can you tell us more about..." and "How did you feel about that?"

Be aware of the objectives being taught each session. Encourage the information to come from the children before you include education yourself. Emphasize important points before going on to the next picture. Read the sentence on the lower part of the page.

Be aware of the time and the number of pictures to be worked on each session. The time goes quickly!

MOVING ON:
See list of Welcoming activities.

III ENDING

THIS WEEK: Ask for feedback about the session.
Make a brief statement beginning with: "Today, we..."
Keep objectives in mind and what you want to emphasize.

NEXT WEEK: Introduce next general topic by saying, "Next week we will..." Let them know if there is anything they are expected to bring.

SCRIBBLE OUT: The children are usually extremely attentive and well behaved and on their good behavior for 1 1/2 hours. They often release pent up feelings by running and chasing when they leave.

Especially, if you don't schedule an active exercise to release some of this energy, a scribble exercise is needed.

Ask what kind of feelings and energy they still have inside? Close their eyes...what is still stuck inside? What color is it...what shape...size? Can you put it on paper...?

Other scribble activities are suggested with each session.

CREATIVE GOODBYE:
Endings are part of life. Learning to say goodbye helps develop coping skills for separations. There are many ways to say goodbye. Encourage the words as well as creative touching as they get to know each other. Children need hugs. Suggestions are included with each session, but children may have additional ideas. They will want to know when they will meet again and what they will do. You will want them to leave with good feelings and want to return.

UNIT III.

Emotional Impact of Death on Children

A death in the family completely upsets the family equilibrium and causes overwhelming changes creating excessive upheaval and anxiety. It is difficult for a child to mourn until they feel secure, and because of their parent's own personal grieving this may not occur until several years after the death. Children may mirror the feelings and behavior of grieving adults, but it is also possible that their grief may come out in the form of anger or boisterous behavior.

Too often, adults avoid talking to children about death, and children get the message that death is a taboo subject. If they don't receive a clear explanation about the cause of death, they may blame themself or worry needlessly about developing cancer or heart problems themselves when they don't feel well.

When a child's parent dies, the child will naturally be concerned how his or her needs will be met and will worry about the surviving parent. The younger the child, the greater the dependency needs are but it is common to see a child become compulsively self reliant or very narcissistic. This can lead to relationship difficulties as an adult if they don't learn to recognize abandonment fears.

The death of a sibling is another traumatic experience which often promotes excessive guilt. Children need to know that angry thoughts and wishes are part of most normal loving relationships.

Periods of hyperactivity, low frustration tolerance, angry outbursts, shortened attention spans, increased fearfulness, and nightmares can be normal symptoms for a grieving child, but persistant problems require professional intervention. Some clinicians (Kliman, Krupnick, E. Furman) recommend at least some timelimited intervention for all children who lose a parent.

TASKS OF GRIEVING
(Sandra Fox 1985)

1. UNDERSTANDING. Accepting what has happened is real.

2. GRIEVING. Working through the many feelings that are part of the grief process.

3. COMMEMORATING. Rituals and other ways to publicly recognize the loss and remember the person.

4. MOVING ON. Permission to focus on life again.

Children's Concepts of Death

Studies in cognitive development suggest general grief response by age. This is offered as a rough guide because many children who experience the death of a parent or sibling seem to comprehend more than these early studies suggest.

PIAGET'S PRE OPERATIONAL LEVEL (ages 2 1/2 - 6)

A child attributes to the dead all of the qualities they had in life such as eating, sleeping, playing, working in a big box in the sky. A child this age assumes everyone feels the same emotions he/she feels. They often see causes of death based on fiction or safety warnings. Based on Maria Nagy's work in 1948, Grollman writes that children 3-6 may view death with a false sense of power over another's life. Children often have formed unrealistic associations for the cause of death, and there is a need to detect misconceptions that create anxiety. Children ages 5-6 have difficulty comprehending finality of death. They do mourn, but differently than adults. They are more likely to "act out feelings" because they do not have the vocabulary to verbalize grief.

PIAGET'S CONCRETE OPERATIONAL LEVEL (AGES 7 - 10)

Children see death as final, but occurring to others. They think they can hide or run from death. Between the ages of 7 and 9, Nagy observes that children see death as a person in the form of a "bogeman", skeleton, or ghost, etc. that can catch you and carry you away. They associate death with the old, but are beginning to see it as real...to others! They associate death with disintegration of the body, and are very interested in details of burials and funerals. It is difficult to understand "death" until a child has had enough experience with the world to know what "alive" is.

PIAGET'S FORMAL OPERATIONAL LEVEL (ages 11 on)

Children begin to express the emotions and intellectual process more as an adult would. Most children are able to formulate realistic concepts based on biological observation. It is the beginning of anticipating their own death.

Developmentally Appropriate Death Education

From the earliest school years, a child can be expected to understand basic concepts of death if it is presented in a factual way.

CONCEPTS AND OBJECTIVES APPROPRIATE FOR ELEMENTARY AGES

A. AWARENESS OF FEELINGS

1. To explore the abstract realm of feeling.

2. To recognize that emotions can be expressed in various ways.

3. To recognize that both happy and sad feelings are a normal part of living.

B. PHYSICAL BODY AWARENESS

1. To identify unique body functions.

2. To identify body changes after death.

C. BODY AND SPIRIT

1. To explore the relationship of the spirit of a person and the physical body.

D. LIFE CYCLES

1. To discuss how growth and change occur naturally.

E. CAUSES OF DEATH

1. To understand simple physical causes of death.

2. To reduce perception of self blame.

3. To recognize that living goes on despite the grief caused by death.

F. GRIEF EXPRESSION

1. To recognize that the feelings of sadness, loneliness, anger, guilt, fear, etc. of grief are normal.

2. To develop ways to express grief and receive support.

3. To reflect on past losses.

BY JUDITH VIORST

How Do You Talk To A Child About Death?

A pet dies. A grandparent dies. A parent, sibling or friend dies—and your child is hurting, frightened, confused and filled with questions. Here, wise advice on how to talk to children about this most sensitive subject.

Katie's gerbil, Sugar, suddenly died a couple of days ago. Katie was devastated. Mortality had hit close to home at last. She wept and clung to her mother and tried to make sense of a baffling world in which death could strike anywhere, anytime—and so fast. But wait! Could Sugar have died because she—Katie—had somehow failed to take proper care of him? Certainly not, said her mom. Then Katie asked, "Why?" And wasn't it unfair that Sugar, such a lovable, never-hurt-anyone creature, had to die?

A gerbil dies. A pussycat dies. A grandfather dies. A grandmother dies. Sometimes a parent or brother or sister or classmate dies. Most of our children will be confronted, in some form or another, with mortality. How do we, their parents, help them cope with their questions and feelings? How do we talk to our children about death?

In earlier times, when folks died at home, death was a part of life—familiar to adults, familiar to children. But in the 20th century, we banish our dying to hospitals and death to the farthest reaches of our minds. In recent years, Elisabeth Kubler-Ross, M.D., author of *On Death and Dying* (Macmillan), and other specialists have encouraged us to look at and talk about death—to ourselves and to each other. And, when it's time, to talk about death to our children.

It's time to talk about death to our kids when they first start asking us questions—and, in the normal course of events, they will. "For everywhere," notes Frances Millican, M.D., a supervising and training analyst with the Washington Psychoanalytic Institute in Washington, D.C., "children encounter evidence of death." Their questions may arise, as my sons' questions first arose, when they see a dead squirrel on the road ("Will I get dead too?") or when they step on an insect ("When will it get alive again?") or when they pass a cemetery ("What's in there?"). And their questions will intensify when they occasionally experience the deaths of pets or people they know.

"Teaching kids about death," says Dr. Millican, "is very much like teaching them about sex." Which means, she says, that as their questions come up, we should try to answer them in a way that is keyed to their age and understanding. And which also means that, just as we may supplement talks about sex by providing our children with solid books on the subject, so we may want to use children's books to supplement our discussions with kids about death.

Although it is surely important, when discussing death with our children, to speak to them at their level of comprehension, it is also important, the experts say, not to be evasive, or to give them explanations of death that we ourselves do not accept or believe. Furthermore, in the excellent book, *Explaining Death to Children* (Beacon Press), Earl Grollman warns there are "unhealthy explanations" that parents should avoid:

So-and-so has gone on a very long journey for a very very long time. (The notion that someone he loves has left him without even saying goodbye could make a child feel angry and hurt and abandoned.)

So-and-so has been taken away by God because he's so good. (This explanation could make a child fear that the reward for goodness is death.)

So-and-so has died because she was sick. (A child may develop fears that the normal illnesses he experiences could kill him.)

So-and-so is in eternal sleep. (Equating sleep with death may lead a child to fear bedtime on the grounds that he might never wake up again.)

Although our religious beliefs may be a part of our discussions of death with our children, child psychoanalysts say that we shouldn't confuse our kids by fudging the facts of death. In other words, says Robert Gillman, M.D., a child psychoanalyst with the Baltimore–Washington Psychoanalytic Institute in Washington, D.C., and president of the Association for Child Psychoanalysis, "Even if we tell our children that Grandpa's soul is in heaven—if that's our belief—we first should make it very clear that his body is in a coffin in the ground."

Erna Furman, a child psychoanalyst with the Cleveland Center for Research in Child Development and the Hanna Perkins Therapeutic School in Cleveland, Ohio, and author of *A Child's Parent Dies* (Yale University Press), has concluded from years of work that an "avoidance of the realities does not protect children but may add to their fears." If children are not given clear information, notes Furman, who trained in psychoanalysis under Anna Freud, "they will make up their own answers, which are usually very mixed up and much more frightening."

What realities, then, can we offer our children? Mrs. Furman suggests that we might respond to a child who asks us, "What is dead?" by linking the questions to something familiar: "Remember that dead bird you saw last week?" We then could go on to say, "That bird wasn't eating. It wasn't flying. It wasn't scared of us. It didn't feel pain." Children as young as two, she says, can grasp this information, although they may have trouble accepting the fact without adult help that death is irreversible.

Young children up to age nine or so may know that there is death in the world without really grasping that death is universal. But sometimes a contact with death will make them fearfully wonder, "Could this happen to me?" And when they ask such questions, says Dr. Gillman, "you answer honestly. You do not lie." However, he notes, it's not necessary to focus on the fact that they're going to die. Instead, he suggests we might say, "You are going to live for a very long time—until you're very old." And then, if they continue on to the logical next step and ask, "But when I'm very old, *then* will I die?" we should answer, "Yes, *all* living things die."

We might find it helpful, when children ask these questions, to read them a sweet, simple picturebook called *Lifetimes: The Beautiful Way to Explain Death to Children* by Bryan Mellonie and Robert Ingpen (Bantam). In talking about different lifespans—a few weeks for butterflies, over a hundred years for certain trees—the book gently makes the point that, "there is a beginning and an ending. In between is living."

Ideally, we'll first discuss death with our kids in the course of daily events, before they are suddenly faced with a painful loss. But at some point we may have to tell a child the shocking and sorrowful news that someone he cares for is dying—or is dead. We can help a child to brace himself, *(continued*

How Do You Talk To A Child About Death?

continued from page 32

Mrs. Furman suggests, by first saying, "I have something very sad to tell you." Dr. Gillman adds that breaking such news is best done in familiar surroundings and that we try, despite our own grief, to hug and comfort our child.

Mrs. Furman points out that a child may need help in "distancing himself from the fate of the dead." A parent might say, she suggests, that "Mr. X died because he was very old and had a sickness that only very old people get. This cannot happen to you or to mommy or daddy. We are much younger and expect to live for a long, long time."

But even in tougher cases—as when a young child loses a mother or a father—it is possible for an adult to help allay his fears, to help him in the "distancing" process. Mrs. Furman tells about Jenny, age three when her mother died, who was full of anxious questionings about whether she and her siblings and dad would die too. She also refused to be her doll's mommy. But her father, says Mrs. Furman, was able to gently lead her to the view that, as Jenny put it, "Most mommies don't die. I'll get big and I'll be a mommy and a grandma and then I'll wear a shawl like my grandma."

When confronted with a death, a child needs our help not only with the initial shock, but also later on, as he faces a host of confusing and complex emotions. Anger. And guilt. And sorrow. And sometimes a desperate and poignant denial—a refusal to face the fact that the dead are dead.

Denial, mental health experts agree, is a normal first response to news that is too painful to assimilate. Mrs. Furman talks of one child, three-and-a-half-year-old Bess, who knew that her mother was dead but who nevertheless announced one night that, "Mommy called and said she'd have dinner with us." Mrs. Furman quotes the father's wise response, which both acknowledged his child's painful yearning and helped her come to terms with death's finalities. "I think you wish mommy would call and have dinner with us," he said. "When we miss mommy so very much we'd like to think that she is not really dead."

Parents can also help their children deal with the anger that follows a loved one's death. Consider, for example, the seven-year-old whose oldest sister died in an auto accident. The boy was furious! Furious at the girl who was driving the car. Furious at his sister because she rode in the car. And furious at himself for *letting* her ride in it. Just . . . furious. To help a child deal with such anger, says Dr. Millican, a parent should begin by "acknowledging it. You tell the child the truth—that you're angry too. You agree that life isn't fair because the fact is, sometimes life just isn't fair." And after his anger is given its due, a parent can begin to say, "But she died. It happened. We have to accept it."

Guilt too is a common response to a death—"I should have taken better care of my gerbil" or "I should have kept my sister out of that car." We can reassure a child who has lost his gerbil—as the father so tenderly does in the comforting storybook *Petey* by Tobi Tobias (G.P. Putnam's Sons)—by pointing out, "You've taken such good care of him," and "Honey . . . think what a great time he's had with you . . . all the talking and playing and loving." The boy who suffers from guilt because he did not save his sister needs to be told, Dr. Millican says, that nobody—neither a little boy nor a grown-up—can possibly have the power to control all that happens in someone else's life.

A child may also suffer a lot from the secret guilt and fear that someone has died because . . . he wanted that person dead—because he harbored some angry, nasty, murderous feelings toward him. Mrs. Furman says that parents can help by letting their children know that even the angriest, nastiest feelings can't kill—that "people don't die because someone wishes it."

"Remember how much, how very much she loved you," I reminded my children after my mother died.

As for the sorrow that children feel at the death of someone they love, analysts say we have to permit them to feel it. Yet many parents find it hard to sit with a child's sadness. They want to remove his pain, immediately. But it doesn't help a child to say, "Hey, it isn't really so terrible," or "Don't cry, sweetie, we'll buy you a new cat tomorrow." We need to accept his pain. We need to allow it, share it, empathize with it. And by crying with him, or encouraging him to talk about his feelings, or giving him an "I understand" wordless hug, parents can let a grieving child know that sadness is permissible, and survivable.

Rituals and ceremonies can help a child mourn a death, the experts say. A funeral for a dead pet, for instance, can give a child a chance to weep and remember. In my own book, *The Tenth Good Thing About Barney* (Atheneum), a little boy remembers that his dead cat, Barney, "was brave. . . . And smart and funny and clean. Also cuddly and handsome, and he only once ate a bird."

The psychoanalysts and clergymen I talked with also encourage parents, when possible, to include the children in funerals and memorial services. They say that participating in all or part of such rituals can help to make the death real for them, can help them to remember and honor the dead, and can help them—by seeing and sharing in the emotional reactions of the group—to understand that they are not alone. Mrs. Furman adds, however, that children younger than six might best stay at home if a parent can't be with them both physically and emotional-

ly, or if the service will be too long or difficult, or if the people attending the service are expected to be emotionally out of control. But we still should include them, she recommends, by telling them about the funeral ahead of time and again when we come home.

Just as children need help in dealing with their fears and confusions, they also need help in adapting to a death. As part of that adaptation, a child may identify with some positive aspect of the person who died. Such identifications, which a parent might want to encourage, give the child something to keep while he is also learning to let a loved one go. Mrs. Furman tells of a four-year-old girl whose father reminded her that her mother, who had died, had liked to feed birds. "You liked that too," he said. "Let's put out a bird feeder. That's a happy way to keep mommy with us."

We can also help a child to adapt by encouraging him to recall good memories of the person who has died. In *Nana Upstairs and Nana Downstairs* by Tomie dePaola (Putnam), four-year-old Tommy finds comfort, after Nana dies, in remembering what Nana looked like, and the stories she always told, and the candy and companionship and other good things that he and Nana shared.

It helps a child to talk about such memories.

"Remember how Grandma Ruth took you to see the deer?" I reminded my children after my mother died. "Remember how you went with her for hamburgers at Don's, and then to pick out a toy at Valley Fair? And remember," I always added—hoping the knowledge would always dwell in them somewhere—"remember how much, how very much she loved you."

Many parents find it painful to speak of death and dying with their children. Many are also afraid that they'll say the wrong thing. But Mrs. Furman notes, "You don't have to be perfect. Parents can make mistakes—and then correct them." She also believes that a parent who finds it hard to talk about death could tell her child, "This is hard for me—but I'm trying." She says that a parent could also tell her child that she hopes that by talking about it together, "it won't be as hard for you as it is for me."

Mrs. Furman says that children respect this kind of honesty. Such talk is good for them, and it's good for *us* too. For, as Mrs. Furman notes, whenever adults help children deal with death, "they invariably will find some help for themselves." ●

Judith Viorst's latest book is *When Did I Stop Being 20 and Other Injustices* (Simon & Schuster, 1987). She lives in Washington, D.C., with her husband, Milton, who is a political writer, and their three sons, Anthony, Nicholas and Alexander.

"GRIEVING AND GROWING"
COMMUNITY COALITION FOR GRIEF SUPPORT

Dear Parent,

You can reserve a place for your child/children in our next young people grief support group by filling in the enclosed registration form and returning with a $10 materials fee for each child.

Groups will be offered for children ages 6-12 and Teens 13-18 as needed at the same location the ADULT GRIEF SUPPORT GROUP meets. Activities for young people are designed to help them understand and express feelings as well as provide an opportunity for them to share with others in a similar situation.

Children ages 6-12 use the workbook, WHEN SOMEONE VERY SPECIAL DIES by Marge Heegaard. They will illustrate the book with their personal story as they express symbolically their ideas, feelings and perceptions. The workbook is designed to teach basic concepts of death and the grief process. Young people are more comfortable communicating with pictures than words.

Most children are apprehensive about attending a support group the first time. We suggest that you request them to come once and then decide for themselves if it something they want to continue. Most children are very eager to return!

We provide a simple snack and beverage the first session. After that the children take turns bringing something for the group. We prefer something simple and low sugar content. You may sign up the first session for a day that is convenient for you.

What helps children most is for you to understand, accept and be able to express your own grief. We strongly urge you to attend the support group for adults at the same time and location. There is no fee for the adult group and it meets throughout the year at an Edina church, Thursdays at 4:30-6:00. You can call Bev Maxwell at 929-5788 for more information.

Additional information about the groups will be available the first session. Signs will be posted with directions to find the meeting rooms.

We look forward to meeting you and providing this opportunity for your child during this difficult time. Facilitators have been trained to understand childhood grief. Some have had a similar experience when they were young. They all volunteer their time because they care.

Very sincerely,

Marge Heegaard

Marge Heegaard, MA, ATR, LICSW

COMMUNITY COALITION FOR GRIEF SUPPORT

CHILDREN'S GRIEF SUPPORT GROUP

WHEN SOMEONE VERY SPECIAL DIES

Confidential Background Information:

Participating child's name: Birthdate:

Date of Death:

Parent(s):
Address:
Phone:

Other Siblings:

Please describe the circumstances of your family's loss.

Briefly describe your child's adjustment before, during, and since this crisis:

Feel free to share with us any thoughts, feelings, or information which you believe might facilitate your child's participation in our group.

RETURN FORM AND $10 MATERIALS FEE TO RESERVE A PLACE FOR EACH CHILD
TO: Marge Heegaard 99 Woodland Circle, Edina, MN 55424

CHILDREN'S GRIEF SUPPORT GROUP EVALUATION

NAME OF
PARTICIPANT_____AGE_____
(Fill one sheet per child)

TYPE OF LOSS_____DATE OF LOSS_____

DATE OF GROUP_____NUMBER SESSIONS_____

PARENT/S NAME_____

ADDRESS_____
            City   State   Zip
PHONE NUMBER_____HOME_____WORK

Was your child **EAGER** or **RELUCTANT** to attend first session?
(circle)
Did your child **ENJOY,DISLIKE,**or **MAKE NO COMMENTS** about the group?
(circle)
How did you learn about the group?_____

How did your child express feelings before this group?

Has this changed since participating in the group?

Have you noticed behavioral or emotional changes since
participating?

Have other commented about changes or problems? (teachers,
friends, etc.)

Was this a positive or negative experience for your child?
Please share.....

Do you have suggestion to improve this service for children?

Curriculum: When Someone Very Special Dies

This book was designed to teach children death education, to recognize and express feelings of grief, encourage open communication, and help adults discover unhealthy misconceptions the child may have. The concepts needed to teach the following objectives are included in the following text, but may be stressed further by additional reading suggested.

SUPPLIES BOX   (BRING WEEKLY)

```
1   WORKBOOK per child
1   BOX OF 8 CRAYONS  per child
12  SHEETS 8x10 NEWSPRINT per child (scribble sheets)
1   8x10 FIRM WHITE PAPER per child (name tags)
1   8x10 COLORED CONSTRUCTION PAPER (for group rules)
    SMALL BOXES OF COLORED PENCILS ( 10-12 year olds )
    PAPER TOWELS (for spills)
    SCISSORS
    BOX OF KLEENEX
    EXTRA SNACK & PACKAGE OF LEMONADE (in case a child forgets)
    EXTRA CUPS AND NAPKINS
```

ADDITIONAL

```
WEEK I.    SNACK AND BEVERAGE
           CUPS AND NAPKINS
           FACILITATOR PICTURES FOR INTRODUCTION
           BOOK FROM LIST FOR INTRODUCTION


WEEK II.   (CHILDREN BRING BABY PICTURES)
           VOLTIVE CANDLE AND MATCHES
           BOOK  FROM LIST FOR INTRODUCTION


WEEK III.  BOOK FROM LIST FOR INTRODUCTION


WEEK IV.   POPSICLE STICK per child
           BOOK FROM LIST FOR INTRODUCTION


WEEK V.    TAPE PLAYER AND OPERA OR LIVELY MUSIC TAPE
           CAMERA AND FILM IF POLAROID IS NOT AVAILABLE NEXT WEEK
           BOOK FROM LIST FOR INTRODUCTION


WEEK VI.   1 SHEET WHITE PAPER 18"x24" FOR CLOSURE
           6 3" CIRCLES COLORED CONTRUCTION PAPER per child
           CANDLES FOR CUPCAKES
           MATCHES
           CHILD SCISSORS
           POLAROID CAMERA OR PRINTS FROM LAST WEEK
           BALOONS (optional)
           BOOK FROM LIST FOR INTRODUCTION
```

WHEN SOMEONE VERY SPECIAL DIES

SESSION I

CHANGE IS PART OF LIFE p.1-6
See change as a natural part of growth
Discuss personal change/losses
Identify ways of coping with change
Discuss changes related to death

A. BEGINNING

SNACK: Provide a snack yourself the first session, or ask someone to bring one. Have parent or child sign up to bring something for the remaining sessions. The child serves.

SCRIBBLE IN: Using newsprint, ask the children to draw very quickly the "ugliest picture" they can draw. Welcome them to a group that is going to be different from anything they have gone to before. They will be doing a lot of art, but it will be different than at school. They will not be doing pretty pictures for the wall or refrigerator. It will be art used to tell a story.

GATHERING:

Fold a 9x12 paper lengthwise, and ask the children to print their first name...and then decorate their "name plate" with pictures of things they like to do, or are interested in. When they finish, guess what their interests are, and when someone guesses correctly...everyone can say (name) likes _____. Keep the names where everyone can see them.

Welcome them all. Note that there are some similarities and some differences in their interests. Acknowledge that they all have one thing in common. They are all part of this group because they have all had someone very special die.

Ask if they know what a grief support group is, and how they feel about coming. Ask for honest feelings because that is what this group is all about. Explain that it is a place where they can learn more about death and the feelings that they feel. Discuss group rules.

B. CONTENT

INTRODUCTION:

Introduce self. I like to do this by bringing about six pictures of myself and families I have been part of (early childhood, high school, college, wedding, first family when they were young, second marriage wedding picture and recent wedding when youngest son was married). I tell them my first husband died when my boys were 8, 10, and 12.

Some of the pictures show personal interests, and they can see how interest change with age, how people change, and how families change. They also get to know you quickly. "Today we're going to be illustrating a book that will be a story about the changes in your family."

Page 1.
"Change is part of life." I can show you how to draw something very easy to begin your book. You can draw a very tiny O for an egg. You can connect alot of O's to make a caterpillar.
Next, a LARGE O for a cocoon. Last, drawing 4 O's will form a butterfly that you can color anyway you like.

Page 2.
People change too. Draw a picture of you in the center the way you think you look now. On the left, draw a picture of how you think you looked when you were a baby. How were you different? How do you think you will change when you get very old? How long would you like to live if you could choose? Discuss. Draw a picture of how you might change (might need glasses...hair might change color...or might fall out...clothes might be different, etc.). (If they draw themselves very young, check for fears of dying early, and fears of aging.)

Page 3.
CHANGE CREATES LOSS. When you were little, you had little losses (crib, bottle, pacifier, teeth, haircuts, leaving Mom to go to school). Do you remember how you felt? Perhaps you had a lot of different feelings. Now you have had a big loss...and you probably have a lot of different feelings. Grief is the word for the feelings that come with loss.

Have you noticed that there are times when you feel very sad...and sometimes not at all. Grief is like that. It is a little like wave in the ocean...they can be so strong that they knock you over. They are powerful and can be frightening. Other times they go away, and come back gently.

Have there been many changes in your life...what is different? Discuss.

People act differently when they lose something important. How do you act when you lose something important? Discuss (denial, anger, cry, replace, feel guilty). They are all normal... some are better for us than others. Discuss.

page 4.

Page 5.

All living things die eventually. Draw as many things that you can think of that can cause death.

Draw...Discuss

What caused the death of your person? (Note if they included it in the causes...also note if the causes are especially violent.)

Read and emphasize that people cannot die because of anything we say or think. Most people get angry at the people they love, and sometimes say they hate them...or wish they would die, but wishes can't make a person die. (More about this comes up later when children feel more comfortable in the group.)

Page 6.

C. ENDING

THIS WEEK: Today we talked a lot about change and loss and a bit about death. Perhaps you have a family album where you can see changes in you and your family.

NEXT WEEK:

You can bring a picture of you when you were little. Who will bring a snack to share? We talked a little about death today, and next week we'll talk about it somemore, and about funerals.

SCRIBBLE OUT:

You have been sitting a long time. Before you leave, let's get some pretend exercise. Choose a color you like...and draw some big circles... imagine you are running around and around! Follow or chase another color, next run in any direction you'd like...and maybe jump up and down. How could you do that on paper? Or kick a ball? Or swing a bat? How does that feel? Perhaps not as good as actually running...but your mind had a chance to run.

CREATIVE GOODBYE:

I'd like to know how you felt about our time
together today (feedback). How do you feel about
coming next week? I've enjoyed getting to know
all of you...(list names). Our time is up, and it
is time to say goodbye for this week. How do you
like to say goodbye? (Discuss) The words
"goodbye" mean "God Be With You." Today, let's
say goodbye to each one. (Facilitator
start...Goodbye X, X, X, X, & X. Person next to
her does the same thing and so on.)

SESSION II

DEAD IS THE END OF LIVING p.7-11
Learn basic concepts of death education
Assess understanding of cause of death
Identify personal misconceptions
Accept reality of loss

A. BEGINNING

SNACK: The child that brings a snack serves it and cleans up after.

SCRIBBLE IN:
Can you quickly draw some changes that you noticed this week. We'll see if we can guess. Or: Choose a color you don't like, and make a scribble mark on your paper. Pass the paper to the right and try to turn what they didn't like into a picture. Pass around allowing each child to add a few changes. When finished and returned ask them how they like it...and encourage honesty. O.K. to not like it.

GATHERING:
My name is (   ) and this is how I looked when I was little. OR, My name is (   ) and the change I noticed this week was...

B. CONTENT

LAST WEEK: Last week we talked about loss and change...etc.

TODAY:
Today we're going to talk about death and funerals. (film or book on death can be read)

Page 7. Read sentence on top of page. Can you draw a picture that would tell why your special person died...

Draw...DISCUSS

(Note how much they know about the cause of death, and how much they understand it. This is important. They need to know it isn't something that could easily happen to them, or others. Children fear getting the same thing. Children need more explanation about the disease or accident than they usually get. (Perhaps they need an explanation by their pediatrician.) Children can often draw and explain cancer better than I can!

Read sentence at bottom of page, and discuss. Ask if the death seems real...or like a bad dream. Young children seem to understand that death is permanent better than research claims.

Page 8.   Light a candle. Comment on the warmth, light, special quality. Blow it out. Ask where they think the warmth, light, and special quality went. Does the candle still seem the same? Explain that people have something special too...it is the warm, loving, caring part of them and it is called a spirit or soul. When someone dies, it leaves the body.
                 Did you see your special person after they died? How was that for you? How did they look? Was the body placed in a casket...or cremated.
                 DRAW ANYTHING YOU WOULD LIKE TO ON THIS PAGE.

                 Draw...Discuss

Some adults think the body looks like an empty shell after death. Some think people look like they are sleeping, but death is not at all like sleeping. Many people don't like to see someone after they die. That could be because then they know for certain they are dead...and no one likes that! Sometimes, when a person has had cancer and has changed a lot before they die, it helps to see them once more the way they used to look.

Page 9.   Read sentence at top of page.

                 Draw...Discuss

Children generally draw the cemetery if they have already drawn something about the funeral on the page before. It is important to find out if they feel they had a chance to say goodbye. If not, they need to find a way to do so.
(letter...another trip to the cemetery, etc.)
Discuss the kind of day...who was there...did people cry...how did they feel...Did they get support from others...or was the family busy with adults.

Page 10.   Read.   Draw what they think.

                            Draw...Discuss

                Sometimes it is hard for adults to admit there is
                something that they have no answers for.   Faith
                can be called believing in the unknown.   Children
                can be very angry that prayers were not answered
                in the way they asked.   They can be mad at a God
                that others told them took their loved one away.
                I think it is healthy to be aware that people have
                different belief systems.   Some facilitators may
                treat this page differently.   I have found this
                section open to adaptation by persons of varied
                faith communities.   It is important to allow and
Page 11.   respect different beliefs from your own.

                There are things I wonder about...DRAW...SHARE

C. ENDING

THIS WEEK: Today we talked about death and funerals, and how
                difficult it is to say goodbye to someone we love.

SCRIBBLE OUT:
                The things we talked about today probably stirred
                up some sad feelings...things you think you would
                not have to think about.   Yet, we're learning that
                it is not good for our body to let sadness get
                stuck inside.   Take a blue crayon and try coloring
                out some sadness.   Color softly and smoothly, and
                see if you can feel sadness flow out through your
                hands.

CREATIVE GOODBYE:
                Turn over name tags, and see how many can say
                goodbye remembering everyone's name.   (The purpose
                of saying goodbye in group is to teach a healthy
                pattern for separations.)

LIVING MEANS FEELING p.12-18
Learn that all kinds of feelings are o.k.
Begin to recognize/name basic feelings
Encourage acceptance/sharing of feelings
Identify ways to express negative feelings

A. BEGINNING

SNACK: As before

SCRIBBLE IN:
Feelings can be expressed with color. Experiment
with your crayons and decide which colors are best
to express anger, sadness, jealousy, fear, and
happiness. What kinds of lines express the same
feelings. Colors chosen will vary because of
associations.

GATHERING:
Each person draws a circle...and puts in a face
with a feeling. Guess. When correct, group
replies (name) are you feeling _____? Child
answers yes or no.

B. CONTENT

LAST WEEK: Last week we talked about death and funerals. Did
you learn anything new?

TODAY:

Today we're going to learn about all these
feelings we have when someone dies. But let's
begin with every day kind of feelings.

Page 12.   Read a sentence at top of page. Ask them to draw
faces that show appropriate feelings. They can
add hair if they like.

DRAW...SHARE

Page 13.   Sometimes people put on a "mask" to hide feelings
they don't like.... It is a good time to discuss
defenses. Acting one way and feeling something
else. This builds a wall that interferes with how
we relate to people. We don't seem real. It is
like wearing a mask. adults that are scared often
act angry. Discuss.
How do bodies act with the different
feelings? Children like to act out feelings, if
there is time. If a polaroid camera is available,
it is fun and helpful to use.

Page 14.   Feelings are something we feel in our body. Begin
            with a blue crayon. Close your eyes and think of
            something very sad (perhaps the funeral). Where
            do you feel that in your body? Color it in on the
            page...a little or a lot whatever you feel.
            Everyone feels feelings in different places and
            different amounts so your pages will all look
            different. Next, black. Think of a scary dream
            you have had. (And so on through all the colors
            listed.)

                        SHARE

            They may want to talk about what triggered the
            different feelings. This is good if it is grief
            related, but otherwise keep the focus on feelings,
            not events. Note that everyone has a different
            amount of feeling...and different locations.
                 Ask which feelings are O.K. (all). Ask which
            feelings are more difficult to express. There
            will be more time to think about those feelings in
            this group.
                 (Look for excess anger, fear, and guilt. It
            shows up in this more than in words. Lack of
            color suggest denial or repressed feelings, and
            they need help. Inappropriate colors or colors
            all scribbled over the entire picture suggest
            confusion with feelings. Very definite and
            controlled coloring suggest controlled feelings.
            (There will be a change in this at the end of the
            group.)

Page 15.   If feelings are stuffed inside...READ....DRAW...

                        SHARE

                 Suggest that if they keep a lot of feelings
            in one place (like head, back, or stomach) they or
            their body may ache there...and that is why it is
            good to let feelings out in some O.K. way.
                 When children are little it is natural to
            want to hit and kick when they are angry, and they
            feel feelings in their hands and feet. When you
            get older you learn that you cannot do that, and
            feelings get stuffed further in.

Page 16.   Draw a picture that the title could be "Something
            Sad" (They will usually draw a picture of the
            cemetery or the funeral...and there is a place for
            that later. I like to find out what makes them the
            most sad now....So I say....Where or when do you
            feel most sad...can you draw a picture of that.)

DRAW...SHARE

Ask them how it felt to draw about this. Ask them
what they usually do when they are feeling
sad...and if it helps. Encourage them to draw,
color, write poetry, write in a journal when they
are feeling sad. It is also important to find
someone they can talk to about sadness. CRYING
HELP TOO...NORMAL FOR BOTH BOYS AND GIRLS!

Page 17.   Sometimes I get angry...(to read is usually enough
              direction).

SHARE AND DISCUSS

(The source of anger varies greatly. They need to
know that anger is normal and O.K. and needs to be
expressed in a non-destructive way.)

Page 18.   Discuss ways to express anger: sports,
hitting or kicking a ball, running, punching a
pillow, screaming into a pillow or in the shower,
verbally expressing "I am SO mad!", etc.
              Anger often involves a family member. If
there is time, family relationships and
communication may be discussed. Stress that it is
O.K. to get angry at anyone: God, parent,
important person, and even the person who died.

C. ENDING

THIS WEEK: Today we talked about feelings. There are many
feelings after someone dies...not just
sadness...etc.

NEXT WEEK:
              We'll be talking more about feelings next week, and
              learn ways to cope with feelings of fear and worry.

SCRIBBLE OUT:
              Let's make sure we let all our anger out today.
              Take a red crayon and a sheet of newsprint. think
              about someone or something that you feel angry
              about...and scribble real hard on the paper...
              continue as long as you can feel angry. (Some
              will fill the entire page. Others will need
              encouragement to draw more than a few soft lines.
              Assure them that this cannot hurt anyone. Some
              may need to scrunch the paper into a ball and
              throw it at a wall.)

CREATIVE GOODBYE:
              Another common feeling of grief is loneliness. Let's
              take hands when we say goodbye today. How does that
              feel? Not so alone? Goodbye until next week.

SESSION IV

FEELING BETTER p. 19-22
    Identify fears and worries
    Recognize individual strengths
    Increase confidence and self esteem
    Learn ways to communicate concerns

A. BEGINNING

SNACK: Same

SCRIBBLE IN:
                Draw a face to show how you are feeling now...and
                one to show the most difficult feeling you had
                last week. Guess and name the feelings. Accept
                them.

GATHERING:
                Read one of the suggested books on feelings.

B. CONTENT

LAST WEEK: Last week we talked about feelings and how they
            need to be let out in some non-destructive way.

TODAY:
            Today we're going to talk and draw about some of
            the feelings that are more difficult to express.

Page 19.   I feel frightened when...(no further discussion
            needed).

DRAW & SHARE

(Children have many fears and are quick to draw
them. They are often nightmares, storms, bigger
kids, and fears of illness and themselves or
someone else dying. Drawing is very effective
because it gives them a sense of power and
control. They feel less helpless. It is a
technique I use frequently in clinical art
therapy.)

(Accept their fears...don't negate.
Encourage communication.) Ask them what they do
when they are frightened...and if it helps...if
not, what might be more helpful. Discuss
realistic fears and unrealistic fears. It is
normal to be fearful about dying after someone you
love dies...Adults do this also. It will not last
forever. One also learns to appreciate life and
other loved ones more. Encourage them to share
fears with others, and not be ashamed of fear.

Page 20.   I worry a lot about....

                    DRAW & SHARE

(Children draw worries about safety of remaining
parent if one has died, or both if a sibling,
grandparent, or other has died. Sometimes they
draw about financial worries, school, or their own
health.
     Children need to know who would take care of
them in the unlikely event that both parents would
die.
     They need to talk about their worries with
their caretakers. Adults need to know what they
are worrying about so they can be more thoughtful
and reassuring. They can allow the children to
call them when they are away, and come home at the
time they are expected.
     Problem solving can be discussed. Children
can be taught to work on problems on paper. They
can list the problems, choices, risks, who can
help and make their decision more clearly.

Page 21.   I feel different because....

                    DRAW & SHARF

     People are all different. We differ in size,
coloring, interests, values, etc. and there are
different kinds of families. Sometimes it seems
as if other families don't have problems, but they
do.
     (Children don't like to be different. There
are many single parent families now, but children
still feel different when a parent dies, or when a
sibling dies, they are sometimes embarrassed.
They worry about crying at school, or feeling sad
when all of their friends seem happy.)
     Children can talk about what they wish they
could change about themselves: size, hair, age,
etc. Next, discuss what they like about themself:
talents, strengths, values.

Page 22.   Something I'm good at....

DRAW & SHARE

Poor self esteem is part of the grief process. it is almost as if they think that even God doesn't like them, or these terrible things wouldn't have happened. It is important to help them feel good about themselves.

There are many ways to express feelings: music (singing or playing an instrument or listening to music), movement (dance, sports, exercise), theater (role playing or acting), writing (journals, poetry, letters) and many visual arts and crafts.

C. ENDING

THIS WEEK:
We have been talking about feelings, and different ways to express feelings.

NEXT WEEK:
Next week we are going to be talking about some memories we have. Maybe you would like to bring a picture of your special person.

SCRIBBLE OUT:
COLOR A SMALL AREA WITH BRIGHT COLORS INTERMIXED, AND COVER WITH THE DARKER COLORS, ENDING WITH BLACK. With a popsicle stick or something, carve through the dark surface to the bright colors (a design, a monster, or lightening, etc.).

CREATIVE GOODBYE:
This has been a good session, and we have learned a lot about each other because we have talked about the things that are important to us. Let's have a group hug to let each other know we think we're all great! Goodbye.

SESSION V

SHARING MEMORIES p.23-27
   Discuss painful memories
   Identify feelings of being responsible
   Recognize losses
   Reinforce positive memories

A. BEGINNING

SNACK: Same

SCRIBBLE IN:
              BRING A TAPE RECORDER AND PLAY A PEPPY TAPE THAT
              THEY CAN COLOR TO. Opera is good because it has a
              variety of moods.

GATHERING:
              Share pictures that they brought of their special
              person. Some are likely to forget, and they can
              tell something about their person.

B. CONTENT

LAST WEEK: Last week we talked about fears and worries. The
              week before we talked about anger and sadness.
              They are all feelings of grief. Grief is the
              natural reaction to the loss and feelings that
              occur when someone dies. Let's think about some
              of the things we have done here. What have you
              liked to do the most..and the least? Discuss.
              These are memories that we now share together. We
              can forget them if we choose...or we can keep them
              as memories.

TODAY: How far back can you remember? What is your
              earliest memory? Can you remember being a
              baby...in a crib? We remember somethings, and
              forget other things.

Page 23.   I remember being told about the death. Where were
              you...Who told you...How did you feel?

                        DRAW & SHARE

                  Discuss feelings more than details. This is
              often the most painful memory. Ask what they
              did...and what others did. Did they get support?
              Did they tell others how they felt? (Generally
              not, and this is why they often don't receive
              support...their feelings don't show.) What could
              they have done to make it better...what could
              others have done. (Encourage children to let
              adults know how they feel.)

-43-

Page 24.   I know how I like to be comforted...DRAW...SHARE

Page 25.   "IF ONLY." People are human, and that means none
             of us are perfect. When someone dies, most of us
             have an "If Only." It is something we wish we did
             or didn't do, said or didn't say. What is yours?

                        DRAW & SHARE

             This is an important page. It is common for
             children to think or tell a parent or sibling that
             they hate them and wish they would die. If
             someone does die, they often have guilt about
             causing the death. Children have magical thinking
             and think wishes have power. They also think (as
             adults do too) that they could have prevented the
             death in some way.
                  This often comes out in their drawing, and
             talking about it eases some guilt. If this
             concept doesn't show up in someone's drawing, it
             should still be discussed.
                  Discuss real guilt and assumed guilt.
             Identify feelings of being responsible. This is a
             pattern that can continue into adulthood and be
             very destructive. Many patterns continue into
             adulthood, and children who feel responsible or
             deny their feelings may need individual therapy.

Page 26.   "My Favorite Memory" What do you remember as the
             happiest time with your special person. Where
             were you? Were others there? Can you put that
             memory on paper...

                        DRAW & SHARE

             It is important to keep good memories, and putting
             it on paper will help you remember this time. How
             did you feel doing this? Did you feel sad
             remembering, and knowing that you wouldn't be able
             to do this again? It is O.K. to feel sad about
             that...it is a big loss. Losses need to be
             grieved. If the sadness is repressed, (stuffed
             inside) the good times may be forgotten too.

Page 27.   "I learned something important from this person."
             It is important to think about what we learned
             from this person. What kind of things did you
             learn...what was the most special...something you
             would like to remember. (I like to discuss this
             before they draw, and encourage them to draw
             something of value. Children have drawn: Be
             brave, Always try your best, Take time to smell
             the roses, etc.)

C. ENDING

THIS WEEK: We've talked about memories today...what we lost, and what we still have. We can always keep what we have learned and the love we received from them.

NEXT WEEK:

Next week you can invite someone from your family to join us. We will talk about families and friends and we will finish our books the first hour. How do you feel about sharing your book with them the last half hour? (Discuss) Then we will celebrate completing this group. Give four balloons (construction paper cut out) to each parent to write something nice about child on each one to bring next week.

SCRIBBLE OUT:

Next week will be our last session. It will be an ending. Can you put your feelings about that on paper?

CREATIVE GOODBYE:

We've talked about the love we have received. Let's share some of that love with each other in a group hug as we say goodbye.

SESSION VI

I'M SPECIAL TOO p.28-32
    Identify support systems
    Describe basic concepts of relationships
    Celebrate completion of book
    Share memories and feelings with family

A. BEGINNING

SNACK: Save for guests.

SCRIBBLE IN:
Have construction paper circles (colors) for each child - as many as in the group. Ask them to write something special about each other in the group. Print each child's name on one.

GATHERING:
Save time for later.

B. CONTENT

LAST WEEK: Last week we shared special memories with each other. We talked about what we had lost and what we still have.

TODAY:

Today we'll talk about the people that care about us, and then we'll share our books with someone from your family. After that we'll have an ending celebration.

Page 28.
I'd like to know more about who is important to you. Draw and name the people you live with inside the house. On the left side of the house, draw your best friend or friends. On the other side, draw anyone that is important to you and is like family but doesn't live with you.

DRAW & SHARE

(This picture shows the support system available to the child. Some have a page full, and others have very little support and need more from the community. Note if they still draw the person that died as part of the family.)
Discuss relationships. What is a family?
(Children Are People teach that families are connected in some way. They share space, money and care about each other. They compete, disagree, and fight with each other but they also help and support each other.)

-46-

You can ask how they relate to each other. Who do they feel closest to, and who, the least close to. Do they tell those they feel the closest to that they care about them? Is there anything they could do to improve the relationship with those they don't feel close to.

Page 29.   "Many people care about me." This shows relationships. Some are close to you like family and relatives. Some are not as close, but are still important like people in the school, churches, hospital and others in the community who care about you too.
       List the people that care about you, and then place that number in the circle showing how close they are to you.

DRAW & SHARE

(Children need to see that there other adults that care about them...and as adults, I think we need to learn to care what happens to all children... not just our own.) (When there is a death in the family, children often lose adults to grief, if not to death.)

Page 30.   I have someone I can always talk to. DRAW...SHARE

       Ask children what makes good friendships? (Sharing, caring, listening, playing, and working together, etc.) Ask them who they can talk to about problems? (Friends, family, relatives, teachers at church and school, counselor, school nurse, doctor, etc.)

Page 31.   "I show others I care about them" Think about the people you care the most about. What do you do to show them that you care about them too?

DRAW & SHARE

Discuss the various ways of showing people that you love and care for them: physical, verbal, helping, presents, time together, etc.

Page 32.   I can still have fun and be happy! (Children need to have permission to be happy when others are sad. Children can't sustain grief for long periods.

DRAW & SHARE

Ask children if there is anything else they would like to talk about before the guests are invited in. Ask again if they feel O.K. about sharing their books. (I never have, but I imagine sometime someone will have a page they would like to remove or cover...and have the right to do so.)

CELEBRATION   Invite guests in, and have each child introduce
              their guest. Serve cupcakes with a candle in each
              of the children's. Say that candles are for
              special occasions and special people. Light each
              candle separately, and pin colored balloons on
              child, reading what is written on each (or have
              parent read).
                   Welcome guests, and to inform them about what
              the group has been doing (and to reinforce concepts
              one more time) tell them that you will go throught
              the books, and they can see and hear a little bit
              about what their child has drawn...but they will want
              to go through it with them at another time more
              slowly with more time for sharing...
                   Allow children to add anything more they
              would like to tell about the group...or what they
              learned from each other.

   PICTURE: Take a polaroid picture of each child if possible
              and mount on a piece of colored construction paper
              that the children can sign. Encourage them to
              keep it on a wall at home with the balloons
              attached with ribbon...to remind them that they
              are special.

   or
   BALLOON: If a camera is not available, get each child a
              balloon printed with, or a card attached saying
              "You are special!"

C. ENDING

   SUMMARY: Thank participants for coming, and what you have
              learned from them..and whatever comes from your
              heart!

   SCRIBBLE OUT: Have a large piece of paper (about 18 x 24) and
              ask children and adults to draw designs and lines
              in many colors...together...without talking...
              until the paper is quite filled...and they feel
              they have expressed caring and good wishes for
              each other.

              Have everyone stand back and look at what they
              have created for a minute or so.

   CREATIVE GOODBYE:
              Suggest they each take a piece home to remind them
              of their time together. One at a time uses a
              scissors and cuts out a piece in any shape they
              would like.

              Again...stand back and look. Put back the piece
              they took out, for a moment...

              Have a group hug including adults, say goodbye and
              gather their piece again, and other momentos and book.

Curriculum: When Something Terrible Happens

This book was designed to use the art process to teach children who have witnessed or experienced a traumatic event some basic concepts about trauma and provide an opportunity to learn about and express related feelings. Misconceptions may be revealed, conflicts resolved and self esteem increased while coping skills are developed. The following objectives are included in the text and can be stressed with additional reading from the suggested books. (Check your local school and public library for titles relating to specific trauma.)

SUPPLIES BOX   (BRING WEEKLY)

```
1   WORKBOOK per child
1   BOX OF 8 CRAYONS  per child
12  SHEETS 8x10 NEWSPRINT per child (scribble sheets)
1   8x10 FIRM WHITE PAPER per child (name tags)
1   8x10 COLORED CONSTRUCTION PAPER (for group rules)
    SMALL BOXES OF COLORED PENCILS ( 10-12 year olds )
    PAPER TOWELS (for spills)
    SCISSORS
    BOX OF KLEENEX
    EXTRA SNACK & PACKAGE OF LEMONADE (in case a child forgets)
    EXTRA CUPS AND NAPKINS
```

ADDITIONAL

```
WEEK I     SNACK AND BEVERAGE FOR GROUP
           CUPS AND NAPKINS
           FACILITATOR PICTURES FOR INTRODUCTION
           PROPS FOR AGE CHANGE INTERESTS (rattle, telephone,
           newspaper, book. hats, wigs, glasses, etc.)
           BOOK FROM LIST FOR INTRODUCTION (optional)


WEEK 2.    CHANGE CARDS WITH NATURE AND PEOPLE PICTURES
           TAPE PLAYER AND RELAXATION TAPE (optional)


WEEK 3.    JAR WITH COVER
           SLIPS OF PAPER WITH FEELINGS WRITTEN ON


WEEK 4.    DEFENSE MASKS (cut from paper or paper plates with binder)
```

```
WEEK 5.    BALL OF COLORED YARN (to toss and braid friendship bracelet)
           TAPE PLAYER AND OPERA OR LIVELY MUSIC TAPE
           CAMERA AND FILM (if polaroid isn't available next week)


WEEK 6.    1  SHEET OF CONSTRUCTION PAPER WITH 13 WORDS WRITTEN
           6  PIECES 2"x3" COLORED PAPER per child
           1  8"X10" SHEET COLORED CONSTRUCTION PAPER per child
           2  GLUE STICKS
           1  SHEET WHITE MEAT WRAP PAPER ABOUT 24"x8' (mural)
              POLAROID CAMERA OR PRINTS FROM LAST WEEK
              MASKING TAPE (to put mural up)
```

WHEN SOMETHING TERRIBLE HAPPENS

SESSION I

SUDDEN CHANGE AND LOSS p.1-5
  Remember life before crisis
  Learn about disaster and trauma
  Acknowledge personal trauma
  Recognize personal losses

A. BEGINNING

SNACK: Provide a snack yourself the first session, or ask someone to bring a simple treat and juice. Have parents sign up to have child bring and serve something for the remaining sessions. Invite the child to serve...it builds self-esteem.

INTRODUCTION:

Introduce yourself. I do this with about six pictures of myself as a child in my original family, pictures in high school and my first wedding. I share that my first husband died and I raised my three boys alone for six years before I married again. I share the picture of my second wedding and our 6 teenagers. They are a wild looking bunch. I share that my new husband was divorced and his wife was unable to take care of her children so they lived with us. Finally I share a recent picture of our family at the youngest child's wedding...and comment on the many changes in my life...and in the children's. The picture shows what fine young adults they all are now. The children seem to love this and bond and develop trust in me more quickly.

Ask them if they know why they are here and how they felt about coming. Ask for honest feelings. Ask them if they know what a grief support group is. After they share their ideas, explain that grief is the word for the many feelings that come with change. This group is a place where they can learn about those feelings and can talk about how they really feel. Everyone is here because something pretty terrible happened. Terrible means fearful or awful. It comes from the word, "terror".

RULES Let the group discuss what rules they would like to have. List on construction paper and keep handy to remind them when needed. (see suggestions for rules in earlier section)

GATHERING:

(NAME TAG) Fold 9x12 paper lengthwise. Invite child to print first name in their favorite color and draw a picture of (1) something they like to eat (2) some-they like to do (3) something they don't like to eat. Explain that just like they learned alot about me from pictures, they can learn about each other. Tell them not to draw too well...so we can have fun guessing what it is. When finished drawing...take turns guessing what the drawings represent.

Keep the name tags out where everyone can see them and learn each other's name

SCRIBBLE IN:

(DRAW AN UGLY PICTURE) Ask them to draw the ugliest picture they can draw. Tell them that in school they try to draw the best they can...but the art here will be different than what they do in school. They will not have many instructions. They will be able to make more decisions themselves. They will be able to draw what they feel like drawing. Begin by drawing what you think is an ugly picture...
                    DRAW...SHARE
Ask them what they think makes their picture ugly. Take a vote for the ugliest picture. Most will draw what they consider an ugly person or alot of scribbles. Tell them scribbles are the way everyone begins to draw. All great artists scribble before they learn to draw. Tell them you think they will learn to have fun with scribbles again. We will have a SCRIBBLE IN and a SCRIBBLE OUT each session.

CHECK IN:
Suggest a weekly check in to share what kind of a week they had, and how they are feeling. Ask for suggestions of how quick scribble drawings could be used. (draw a feeling face each week...or a pot that is full or empty...or a thermometer that is up or down, etc.) Decide which to use each week.

B. CONTENT

INTRODUCTION:

These groups will vary with reasons for children being in the group. Some groups may have children who have all experienced the same trauma such as an earthquake or a tornado. If so, read from an appropriate book for an introduction...but look for a book with many pictures and few words. If the group is made up of children who have experienced a variety of traumas, an appropriate book may be hard to find. It may be more helpful to use the time on the suggested activities.

TODAY:
We are going to talk about the many changes that are a natural part of life.

Page 1.   SOMETIMES THE WORLD IS A WONDERFUL PLACE...Read.
           Encourage children to remember a happy time recently
           or long ago and draw something about the picture that
           comes to their mind.

           TEll them they will have to draw quickly. They won't
           have time to do their best drawing. Just put the
           important things into the picture that will tell a
           little about that time.
                                DRAW... SHARE
           (Ask who would like to begin telling something about
           their picture and what was special about that time?)

Page 2.   THINGS CAN CHANGE SUDDENLY...
                                DRAW...SHARE
           (Children usually have many questions on what and
           how to draw the first pages. I often make suggestions
           on this page on how to draw a tornado   or a
           flood to help them get started. I stress that there
           are many other ways to draw these same things and they
           can do it THEIR way. I often ask them for ideas of
           how to draw an earthquake.)

           It is very important to stress that these things do
           not happen very often.

Page 3.   OTHER TERRIBLE THINGS MAY HAPPEN... read
                                DRAW...SHARE

           (Murder, kidnapping, roberies, abuse, car accidents,
           violent deaths and anything a child considers terrible
           may be drawn Youngest children may not be aware of
           some of these things. Some things are accidental
           and some things are planned.)

Page 4.   SOMETHING TERRIBLE HAPPENED IN MY LIFE...read. Encourage
           children to draw the reason they are in the group.
           (Drawing the fearful event empowers them by letting
           them be in control. The giant overwhelming picture
           in their mind is reduced in size and power when it
           is reproduced on paper.) Some children may choose not
           to draw this page and that must be respected.
                                DRAW...SHARE
           Children are often protected from terrible events
           and may not know details. They may create even
           more terrible fantasies. Misconceptions may be
           revealed.

Page 5.   MY LIFE HAS CHANGED... read.(Encourage children to
           think about what is different. They need to know
           what is different to know what has been lost.)
           Some events will make many life changes and others
           may make few changes. Secondary losses are very
           important: basic trust, security, safety, possessions,
           familiar environment, natural beauty, sense of order
           are just a few examples.
                                DRAW...SHARE

MOVING ON: Divide children into pairs. Have them decide together how they might act out a terrible event without using any words. The others guess what the event is.

C. ENDING

THIS WEEK: We talked about many kinds of events that cause sudden loss and change. Those things don't happen very often. We talked a little bit about something that happened in our life.

NEXT WEEK: We will talk more about that and learn about the many feelings that people feel when something terrible happens.

SCRIBBLE OUT:

(SCRIBBLE PICTURE) On a scribble sheet, draw a big smile with a line across to make a bowl. Draw some lines of different colors coming out. Then use bright colors and alot of different scribbles to make flowers...make many kinds. There are all kinds of flowers. Scribbles can be beautiful! (Encourage them to color hard to get bright colors. They can experiment on the other side with more flowers.

UPS AND DOWNS:

Tell them it is important to be able to learn to share how they feel about what happens in the group. Begin by sharing what they didn't like...anything... what we did or didn't do...what someone said or did. (Respond by thanking them for sharing...no excuses or reasons.

Next, invite them to share what they did like, and again respond with a simple, "Thank you for sharing that."

CREATIVE GOODBYE:

It is important to say goodbye. There are many different ways to say goodbye. Let the group decide how they would like to say goodbye. It should be something similar each time to give them the security of structure. (Some suggestions: goodbye in a foreign language each time, as a group say goodbye to each person in the group, write a goodbye poem and say it each week, taking hands and saying goodbye together, etc.)

Before the group says their goodbye, ask them how they felt about our time together. Ask them if they want to come again next week. (I believe they should be part of the group only if they want to be.)

Say: Our time is up. I've enjoyed getting to know you...and I look forward to next week. It's time to say goodbye now....

SESSION II

GRIEF: A NATURAL REACTION TO LOSS p.6-10
Discover Misconceptions
Discover Feelings of blame
Discuss concepts of criminal justice
Learn concepts of grief

A. BEGINNING

SNACK: The child that brought the snack serves it and cleans up afterwards. This increases self esteem and and decreases feelings of helplessness.

GATHERING: (CHANGING TIME CARDS) Cut out pictures of changes in nature and childhood changes. (seasons, water... ice, etc. crib, bottle, baby sitters, Parent going to work, school, pet loss, funeral, suitcase, house for sale, etc.) Let each child choose a card and share something about the way they felt about that change.

SCRIBBLE IN:

(CHANGING PICTURE) Ask the group to think about a picture they would like to draw...and plan for a few moments how they would like it to look. Invite them to close their eyes and see that picture in their mind. Draw anything they would like...something fun and easy. (always use newprint for scribble in and out activity.)

When they all have a picture pretty well started, say: This is going to be what I call a changing picture...Do you know what that is? Pass your picture to the person on your right. Now, add something to the picture in front of you. Add something that will make it more interesting.

Let them draw for a few minutes...and again say: Stop! Pass your picture to the right. Continue this way allowing about a minute per picture until their original drawing comes back to the original drawer.

Ask them how they feel about the finished picture... Do they like it or dislike it? What are they feeling? Is it changed from the way they imagined it would be?

Change is like that. Everyone has different feelings about what has changed.

CHECK IN: Draw something on the back of the scribble sheet that tells something about what kind of a week they had.
DRAW...SHARE

B. CONTENT

LAST WEEK: We talked about some terrible things that can happen suddenly and violently naturally in nature...and other things that people might do. We talked a little bit about something that happened in our lives.

TODAY: We will talk about that event and try to learn more about what happened and how we feel about it.

Page 6. THE TERRIBLE THING HAPPENED BECAUSE... read. Suggest to them that they probably don't know for sure, but to draw what they THINK.
DRAW...SHARE

(Children may be reluctant to place blame, but it is important to know their thoughts...especially if they blame themself in anyway.)

Some understanding about a particular disaster is helpful. Encourage them to check school and local libraries for helpful books. Education cuts fears.

Page 7. PEOPLE MAY ASK MANY QUESTIONS... READ. (With many traumatic events, police may be involved as well as news people and strangers asking questions. Also, friends ask questions that are hard to answer.
DRAW...SHARE
We have rules for our group, families have rules, schools have rules and there are rules of our world. Time-out is punishment for some rules at home...jail or prison is punishment sometimes when the rules of the world are broken.

Page 8. THE PAIN FROM CHANGE IS CALLED GRIEF...read. (Let children take turns reading. Ask them what it means to them. Ask them what colors would be appropriate for denial...and let them color there. Ask what colors and lines would be appropriate for painful feelings and growth and suggest they color there.

Emphasize that grief comes and goes. It may be strong when it comes back, but it generally won't last as long. Tell them that they will learn how to deal with the difficult feelings in this group.

Page 9. WHEN SOMETHING TERRIBLE HAPPENS IT MAY NOT SEEM REAL AT FIRST... read.
DRAW...SHARE

This is nature's way to protect us from overwhelming feelings. It usually lasts a short time, but sometimes people get stuck here because they are afraid of the feelings. That isn't healthy. Understanding feelings makes them less frightening.

Page 10. OR...PEOPLE MAY HAVE VERY STRONG FEELINGS... read.
DRAW...SHARE

(People in a family often act differently during these
difficult times. Someone may act as if their feelings
are frozen. Someone else may act as if they exploded.
It can be scary to feel or see.

How did you act? How did others act? This is normal.
Feelings and behavior both change.

MOVING ON: (RELAXATION) Use a relaxation tape for children or do
a brief progressive relaxation teaching them to breathe
deeply, tense muscles and relax them.

C. ENDING

THIS WEEK: Today we talked about what happened that brought us to
this group and learned that grief is a natural reaction
to change and loss. We talked a little about feelings.

NEXT WEEK: We will learn more about all kinds of feelings.

SCRIBBLE OUT:
(FRIENDLY CHASE) It isn't easy for two people to
live together. It isn't easy for friends to get
along all the time either. Our scribble out today
will require partners. Identify partners sitting
next to each other. Partners must choose a color
that is different. One will be the leader and
one will be the follower. Decide who will be the
leader. The leader begins to scribble on the
newsprint and the follower follows the same line as
close as possible.

Next...change roles and repeat exercise on other side
of paper.

Ask: Which role did you like best? Follower or
leader? We are all different. Some prefer leading
and some prefer following. What do you have in your
family...leaders...followers...or both? What happens
if everyone wants to lead?

UPS AND DOWNS:
What troubled you today...what did you like?

CREATIVE GOODBYE:
As group decided, but it is important for group
members to say goodbye to each other...not just
the facilitator.

SESSION III

LEARNING ABOUT FEELINGS p.11-15
   Accept all feelings as O.K.
   Recognize and name basic feelings
   Identify repressed feelings
   Discover feeling & behavior relationship

A. BEGINNING

SNACK: As before.

GATHERING: (STUFFED FEELINGS) Copy the list of feelings on a
          sheet of colored paper....Cut them into individual
          pieces of paper and "stuff" into a small jar with
          a cover. Spin the jar and the person it points to
          when it stops picks a paper...and shares a time
          when they felt that feeling. They have the right
          to pass if they choose.

SCARED	NERVOUS	SMART	FURIOUS
BRAVE	SAD	EMPTY	STUPID
LONELY	UNLOVED	DISGUSTED	SPECIAL
CONFUSED	IGNORED	JEALOUS	HAPPY
PROUD	ANGRY	SHAMED	GUILTY
LOVED	AFRAID	EMBARRASSED	WORRIED
CHEATED	EXCITED	FRUSTRATED	SILLY
MISERABLE	BORED	DISAPPOINTED	CLEVER

SCRIBBLE IN:

          (FEELING COLORS) Feelings can be expressed with
          colors. Try different colors and decide which color
          you like best to show anger, fear, sadness, and joy.

          Next...decide what kind of lines express those same
          feelings best. There is no right way. People
          will all choose different lines and colors...but
          some may be similar.

CHECK IN: As decided by the group.

B. CONTENT

LAST WEEK: We learned about and shared some early feelings of grief. We learned that grief is the reaction to loss.

TODAY: We will learn more about many kinds of feelings.

Page 11.   THERE WILLL BE MANY KINDS OF FEELINGS...draw. (Children can do this very quickly and learn the names of feelings they see on other people's faces.) SHARE

Page 12.   SOMETIMES PEOPLE PUT ON A MASK... read. Invite the children to draw three feelings that are difficult for for them to show...and sometimes hide. Ask them to draw the masks or feelings they use to hide them.
DRAW...SHARE

(It is important for them to know that others do this also...so you can't be sure of what a person is feeling by the look on their face.)

Page 13.   FEELINGS ARE SOMETHING YOU FEEL IN YOUR BODY. Begin with anger because it is usually the easiest to identify. Invite children to close their eyes and think of a time´when they were very angry at someone..or something. Someone may have taken something away from you or were mean to you. Where do you feel anger in your body when you think about that time? Use a red crayon and scribble it in at that place on the picture of the body...a little or alot, whatever you feel.

Next...use blue and think of a time when you felt very sad. Close your eyes and decide where you feel sadness in your body...and color that place blue.

Remember a time when you were really scared. Maybe you had a nightmare or maybe it was something else. Close your eyes and decide where you feel that feeling and color it in.

Continue with the other colors. You may need to make suggestions of when they might have felt those feelings. This is an important page and time is required.

(Assessment: With children, I use this mainly to emphasize the need to express feelings to avoid aches and pains in those areas. However, lack of colors suggest repressed feelings. They need to learn that feelings are all O.K. Colors mixed up and scribbled all over suggest confusion or being overwhelmed by many feelings. Coloring very neatly suggest controlling feelings. Parts of the body colored like a patch-work quilt suggest they are unable to identify where they feel feelings.

Page 14.   IF FEELINGS ARE STUFFED INSIDE... Read directions
            and invite them to color any areas they get aches
            and pains.
                            DRAW...SHARE

            Look back at page 13 and see if anger and fear or
            other feelings are felt in the same places they get
            aches and pains. Headaches, stomach aches and back
            aches are often the result of stuffed feelings.

            Hands , feet, and the mouth are natural energy zones
            for feelings. That is why young children bite, hit
            and kick. It is important to substitute acceptable
            behaviors that use the same zones.

Page 15.   WHEN SOMETHING TERRIBLE HAPPENS IT MAY SEEM THAT
            EVERYONE KNOWS ABOUT IT...read.
                        DRAW...SHARE

            Some events become sensational news and children
            may or may not be protected from media. Other
            events may be "unspeakable". No one talks about
            it. Both situations are difficult. Children feel
            self conscious and different. Sharing these
            feelings helps normalize events.

MOVING ON: (FOLLOW THE FEELING PERSON) Invite children to stand
            and stretch. Play a game like "follow the leader".
            Choose an active child to be the first leader and line
            others behind. Invite the leader to act out a feeling
            using both face and body. The others follow and do
            the same thing for a few minutes. The leader goes
            to the end of the line and a new leader begins.

C. ENDING

THIS WEEK: We learned to recognize and name many different feelings
            that might be part of experiencing a terrible event. We
            learned that all feelings are O.K.

NEXT WEEK: We will learn more about feelings and how to cope with
            them.

SCRIBBLE OUT:
            (DRAWING WITH THE NON DOMINANT HAND) Draw a picture
            using the hand you don't usually write with. It can
            be a picture that is timely for this time of the
            year...or it could be about a time when you had a
            strong feeling.

UPS AND DOWNS:
            What made you feel down today...and up today?

CREATIVE GOODBYE:
            As group has decided.

SESSION IV

DRAWING OUT DIFFICULT FEELINGS p. 16-20
Identify angry behavior
Learn ways to express difficult feelings
Identify feelings of guilt
Encourage communication of concerns

A. BEGINNING

SNACK: As before

GATHERING: (ADD-A-LONG FEELING) Begin with...MY FRIEND WAS FEELING_____ BECAUSE_____. The child to the right of you repeats what you said and adds... AND THE DAY BEFORE SHE WAS FEELING_____ BECAUSE_____. Each next person repeats and adds. Continue until someone mixes up and drops out. The last person left wins.

SCRIBBLE IN: (GUESSING FEELINGS) Draw a difficult feeling you felt last week and something about why you felt it. The person who guesses correctly shows their picture next.

CHECK IN: As group decided.

B. CONTENT

LAST WEEK: We learned to recognize and name many kinds of feelings. we learned that if we stuff too many feelings too long, they often cause aches and pains.

TODAY: We are going to talk about some of the more difficult feelings and learn healthy ways to let feelings out.

Page 16. ALMOST EVERYONE FEELS HELPLESS AND ALONE AT CERTAIN TIMES... read.
                    DRAW...SHARE

Children may draw a line down the middle with a lonely time on one side and a helpless time on the other. They feel helpless when they can't fix feelings and things. They need to know children cannot fix adult problems.

Grief is a lonely time. Members of a family have their own grief and are unable to be as supportive. Talking and sharing feelings help people feel less lonely.

Cleaning their room, taking phone messages, and being responsible in age appropriate ways makes a person feel helpful instead of helpless.

-60-

Page 17. MANY PEOPLE FEEL ANGRY WHEN TERRIBLE THINGS HAPPEN...
Read. Encourage children to recognize anger they feel
about this event. They can think about who or what they
feel their greatest anger toward. (This is often siblings.
They have more difficulty admitting anger toward parent.)
DRAW...SHARE

Page 18. WHEN I FEEL ANGRY, I... Read. Encourage children to
draw many different ways they act when they are angry.
DRAW...SHARE

Thank them for sharing. Don't criticize behavior.

Page 19. IT IS IMPORTANT TO LET ANGER OUT IN WAYS THAT DO NOT...
Have children take turns reading the sentances. Suggest
they put a check by the number if it is something they
already do...and a star if it is something they would
like to try.

Invite children to turn back to page 18 and circle the
healthy ways they express anger...and put an X over the
unhealthy ways.

Page 20. SOMETHING SAD...read top line.   DRAW...SHARE

Read lower line. (Note if children draw something
related to the event. Drawing something totally unrelated may indicate denial...but their need for
defenses must be respected.)

Children often associate crying with babies because
babies cry to get their needs met until they learn
words. When a person can talk they are encouraged
to use words to ask for what they need. Crying to
let sadness out is different and is O.K. for every
age.

MOVING ON: (DEFENSE MASKS) Have three masks showing the
feelings of being happy, sad and angry. Pick
two volunteers. Have one act one feeling wearing
a mask...but keeping a different feeling inside.
The other will respond to the actor.

When finished, others may try. Ask them afterwards
how it felt to be the actor...and how it felt to
be the other person. (Masks or defensive feelings
are like walls. They keep you from being close
to the other person. It takes alot of energy to
act differently than you feel.)

C. ENDING

THIS WEEK: We learned some healthy things to do when we feel angry,
lonely, or helpless. We learned that crying when you
feel sad is O.K.

NEXT WEEK: We will learn about memories and other kinds of feelings.

SCRIBBLE OUT:

(SCRIBBLE OUT ANGER) Think about someone you often feel angry at. (This is often a sibling) Draw a symbol or stick person like that person with a red crayon. Think about your anger... put it on the paper by scribbling out the the symbol. Scribble really hard until the anger is all gone. Next, scrunch the paper into a ball and throw it at a blank wall. Finally throw it in a waste basket and try to forget about it. (Children love this. It is a healthy release of anger. They may need to be reminded that this doesn't hurt the person.)

UPS AND DOWNS:

What made you feel down today...and up today?

CREATIVE GOODBYE:

Thank them for sharing and working hard. Say goodbye in the usual way.

SOOTHING PAINFUL MEMORIES p.21-26
Identify fears and guilt feelings
Find power over nightmares
Experience healthy role reversal
Find words for unspeakable events

A. BEGINNING

SNACK: As before

GATHERING: Share a favorite memory...something they remember about
a time when they were happy and having fun.

SCRIBBLE IN: On a sheet of newsprint, have children write the initials
of their first and last name. Add colors and lines to
turn the initials into a picture. They can turn the
paper any direction that works best.

CHECK IN: As group decided

B. CONTENT

LAST WEEK: We talked about difficult feelings and learned O.K.
ways to let them out.

TODAY: We will learn how to talk about some of the difficult
times that are painful to remember.

Page 21.   IT MAY SEEM THAT SOMEONE OR SOMETHING COULD HAVE KEPT
THIS FROM HAPPENING... read. Ask if they can think
or anyone or anything who could have prevented this
thing that happend in their life. Encourage them to
think about that and then draw their answer.
DRAW...SHARE

Page 22.   IF ONLY... read. Tell them that when something like
this happend, most people think of something they
wish they had done differently. Do you have an
"IF ONLY"?   DRAW...SHARE

Page 23.   I REMEMBER WHEN I WAS... read. (Most children do
remember this very well. Some experiences come back
as nightmares. An overwhelming picture in the mind
becomes less powerful when it is drawn and contained
on a small sheet of paper. Nightmares often end
when it has been drawn. This...and the next three
pages are some of the most important in this book.
Allow time. Also respect the child's right to
not draw this page.
DRAW...SHARE

Page 24.   I FEEL FRIGHTENED WHEN SCARY PICTURES COME INTO MY
THOUGHTS OR DREAMS... read. (This is another invitation
to have children draw and verbalize trauma.)
DRAW...SHARE

(Post-traumatic stress occurs following a traumatic
event that is generally outside usual human experience.
The characteristic symptoms involve reexperiencing the
traumatic event, numbing and a variety of symptoms
such as: hyperalertness, sleep problems, guilt about
survival, memory impairment, avoidance and increased
symptoms when exposed to events that symbolize the event.
It may be acute or delayed. Treatment is suggested.)

Page 25.   YOU CAN CHANGE YOUR DREAMS... This is a technique to
empower children to overcome fear of nightmares. Read
DRAW...SHARE

Page 26.   IT IS IMPORTANT TO HAVE A PLACE THAT FEELS SAFE...
Ask them if they have a place that feels safe. If so,
draw it. If not, think of what you would need to feel
safe. What kind of a place would it be? Think about
it and draw it.
DRAW...SHARE

Everyone needs a place to feel safe. Imagery of such
a place is helpful.

MOVING ON: (TALK AND TOSS) Hold a ball of yarn and explain rules.
Only the person holding the yarn can talk. Toss the
ball to a child and share one thing they like about
themself...and then toss the ball across the group to
someone else for their turn. Continue. A web will
be formed. Talk about relationships and connections.
Talk about the need for independence and inter-dependence.
Cut the yarn and give each child pieces to take home
to make a friendship bracelet...or this can be done
in group if there is time.

C. ENDING

THIS WEEK: We talked about some difficult memories that are hard
to forget. It helps to draw those memories and then
talk about it. You have had some scary times. It is
natural to have fears.

NEXT WEEK: Will be the the last session. How do you feel about
that?

We will be talking about things that make us feel good
about ourselves and others. We'll have a celebration
because you have worked hard for this series.

UPS AND DOWNS:
What do you feel down about...what do you feel good about?

SCRIBBLE OUT:
Play a peppy tape in the tape player you brought (opera is good for a variety of feelings). Invite children to use colors and lines to show what they hear in the music. Begin with the dominant hand. After a few minutes suggest they try the other hand. Compare. (the dominant hand is usually less free)

CREATIVE GOODBYE:
Thank them and say goodbye as planned.

SESSION VI

GROWING STRONGER p.27-31
Gain confidence and security
Identify support systems
Recognize personal strengths
Increase self esteem

A. BEGINNING

SNACK: Save snack for ending celebration. (cup cakes preferred)

GATHERING: (Before group begins, print these words on a piece of construction paper: PRETTY, HANDSOME, HONEST, STRONG, FRIENDLY, FUNNY, HELPFUL, CARING, NICE, NEAT, COOL, FOXY, GREAT.) Show sheet to children and ask them which 6 (or whatever the number in the group) they consider the most important. Give each child one of the chosen words to copy on colored slips of paper (about1"x2" the number in the group) and save for the moving on activity.

SCRIBBLE IN: (ROAD MAP OF LIFE) On a sheet of newsprint, draw the ups and downs of your life so far...the road blocks, the bumpy times, the dead ends, the high times, the the bridges. Next, think ahead and draw a road map for your future. What good things do you hope for? Will there still be bumpy times?

CHECK IN: As decided by the group. Also ask how they feel about this being the last session.

B. CONTENT

LAST WEEK: We talked about scary dreams and thoughts. Did anyone have a scary dream last week? Discuss.

TODAY: We will think about something we like about ourselves and learn that there are many people who care about us.

Page 27. SOME PEOPLE BELIEVE...read... DRAW...SHARE

(Younger children may draw parents, some may draw God or an angel. Children who have experienced a traumatic event often have many fears and worry about more bad things happening. They look for and need extra feelings of security. Encourage sharing and respect for different beliefs.

Page 28. I HAVE PEOPLE I CARE ABOUT... read. Encourage them to draw a picture of people who are important to them. (They will usually draw their family. If someone has died , they usually include that person. Sometimes they pull away from loving and caring for fear of losing and hurting.
DRAW...SHARE

Page 29.   MANY PEOPLE CARE ABOUT ME... read. Invite them to list the people who are important to them. Next, place the number in the circle. This is a good time to explain relationships. Some people are close to you like parents and family. Others are not as close to you...you don't see them as often...but they are still important to you. Other grown ups in schools, churches, and other places care alot about children also. (They need to know that many people care about them to feel more secure.)

DRAW...SHARE

Ask them who they can talk to about problems. They can mark that person with a star.

This is a good time to talk about relationships. Caring, sharing and working together makes good friendships. Talk about treating siblings with respect. Encourage them to practice group rules at home as well as in group.

Page 30.   THERE ARE THINGS I LIKE... read. List answers. (Notice how much they can think of on their own on this page. Children with high self esteem will do it quickly. Others need help in discovering their positive qualities. The beginning activity is designed to help this.

SHARE

Page 31.   THOSE WHO LIVE THROUGH TERRIBLE TIMES... read. (Younger children may find this page difficult... even adults find it difficult to see how anything good could possibly come out of terrible events. Yet, it is important to teach positive thinking and it is true something good usually does come along with the bad.

DRAW...SHARE

Page 32.   THIS IS ME...I AM O.K. Read. Encourage them to draw a picture of themself any way they choose.

DRAW... SHARE

(The picture a child draws of themself often indicates how they feel about themself. This final page often is an indication of children who may continue to be at risk for problems... and those who have good coping skills.

MOVING ON: (POSITIVE OBSTACLES) Arrange chairs for a simple obstacle course to crawl under or climb over. Give children a spot to stand and the positive statement slips they made earlier in this session. Take turns going around the course, stopping to recieve a slip from each child as they say, "You are...or are going to be (which ever they choose to say)_____. The facilitator takes the place of the child going around and hands out their slip while they are gone. The children keep their slips to paste on a sheet with the group photo.

CELEBRATION: Serve snack at this time.
Take a group picture using a polaroid camera (or a regular camera the week before and get prints) Have an 8x10 sheet of colored construction paper for the children to glue the picture and the positive words on. Let each child sign their name to the sheet so they will have something to remember their time together.

C. ENDING

THIS WEEK: We have had our 6th and last session. You have worked really hard and I have enjoyed our time together. I feel good about the things you have learned.

SCRIBBLE OUT:
(GROUP MURAL) Before the session begins, draw the grief "wave" from page 8 in the workbook with a black marker on a white piece of butcher paper about 10 ft. long. Tape to a wall. Invite children to decorate the mural with different feelings of grief in appropriate places and appropriate colors and pictures. Decorate as they wish. Suggest they finish by writing O.K. in empty spaces to remind them that all feelings are O.K.

Ask children for permission to keep the mural as a memory of the group and something you might be able to use to teach others about children's grief.

UPS AND DOWNS:
As usual, but allow time for them to express feelings about the group ending. Some may have some sadness or anger. They may choose to have a reunion some time.

CREATIVE GOODBYE:
Suggest a final review of what they have learned together:
Change is a natural part of life.
Change brings feelings of loss and grief.
Sometimes terrible things happen.
Sudden and violent changes are more difficult to cope with
Feelings need to be expressed in healthy ways.
You are important and many people care about you.

Tell them their book will be a reminder of their time here and the things they learned. Encourage them to share the book with their parents because they can learn from it too.

Thank them for being part of the group and for the things you have learned from them. Wish them well and ask them if they would like to say goodbye in a special way. (a group hug is great if they want to. This is another ending for them.)

Curriculum: When Someone Has a Serious Illness

This book was designed using the art process to help children learn some basic concepts of serious illness and provide an opportunity to learn about and express related feelings. Misconceptions may be revealed, conflicts resolved and self-esteem increased while coping skills are developed. It can be used individually or with a group facilitated by a supportive adult educated to accept feelings and encourage communication. Weekly sessions of $1^1/_2$ hours are suggested for each of the six sessions but individual needs may vary. The following objectives are included in the text and can be stressed with additional reading from the suggested books. (Check your local library and book stores for titles relating to specific illnesses.)

SUPPLIES BOX   (BRING WEEKLY)

```
1   WORKBOOK per child
1   BOX OF 8 CRAYONS  per child
12  SHEETS 8x10 NEWSPRINT per child (scribble sheets)
1   8x10 FIRM WHITE PAPER per child (name tags)
1   8x10 COLORED CONSTRUCTION PAPER (for group rules)
    SMALL BOXES OF COLORED PENCILS ( 10-12 year olds )
    PAPER TOWELS (for spills)
    SCISSORS
    BOX OF KLEENEX
    EXTRA SNACK & PACKAGE OF LEMONADE (in case a child forgets)
    EXTRA CUPS AND NAPKINS
```

ADDITIONAL

```
WEEK I    SNACK AND BEVERAGE FOR GROUP
          CUPS AND NAPKINS
          FACILITATOR PICTURES FOR INTRODUCTION
          PROPS FOR AGE CHANGE INTERESTS (rattle, telephone,
          newspaper, book. hats, wigs, glasses, etc.)
          BOOK FROM LIST FOR INTRODUCTION (optional)


WEEK 2.   CHANGE CARDS WITH NATURE AND PEOPLE PICTURES
          TAPE PLAYER AND RELAXATION TAPE (optional)


WEEK 3.   JAR WITH COVER
          SLIPS OF PAPER WITH FEELINGS WRITTEN ON


WEEK 4.   DEFENSE MASKS (cut from paper or paper plates with binder)
```

```
WEEK 5.   BALL OF COLORED YARN (to toss and braid friendship bracelet)
          TAPE PLAYER AND OPERA OR LIVELY MUSIC TAPE
          CAMERA AND FILM (if polaroid isn't available next week)


WEEK 6.   1  SHEET OF CONSTRUCTION PAPER WITH 13 WORDS WRITTEN
          6  PIECES 2"x3" COLORED PAPER per child
          1  8"X10" SHEET COLORED CONSTRUCTION PAPER per child
          2  GLUE STICKS
          1  SHEET WHITE MEAT WRAP PAPER ABOUT 24"x8' (mural)
             POLAROID CAMERA OR PRINTS FROM LAST WEEK
             MASKING TAPE (to put mural up)
```

When Someone Has a Serious Illness

SESSION I

CHANGING TIMES pages 1-6
   Accept change as part of life
   Identify family changes
   Discover personal life changes
   Recognize grief from loss and change

A. BEGINNING

SNACK: Provide a snack yourself the first session, or ask someone to bring a simple treat and juice. Have parents sign up to have child bring and serve something for the remaining sessions. Invite the child to serve...it builds self-esteem.

INTRODUCTION:

Introduce yourself. I do this with pictures of myself as a child, teenager, wedding picture and a picture of my family before my husband died. I share with them that my husband was very sick with cancer for three years before he died. That was 20 years ago and the kind of cancer he had is now very curable. Things were very different then. There were no groups like this. I raised my three boys alone for 6 years and then remarried. I show the picture of our wedding and our six teenagers. No one was too happy about the wedding. Finally, I share a recent family picture taken at our youngest son's wedding. There are many changes! Children like this...it has many examples of family change....and they get to know me quickly.

Ask them if they know why they are here and how they felt about coming. Ask for honest feelings. Ask them if they know what a grief support group is. After they share their ideas, explain that grief is the word for the many feelings that come with change. This group is a place where they can learn about those feelings and can talk about how they really feel. Everyone is here because of a serious illness in their family.

RULES Let the group discuss what rules they would like to have. List on construction paper and keep handy to remind them when needed. (see suggestions for rules in earlier section)

GATHERING:

(NAME TAG) Fold 9x12 paper lengthwise. Invite child to print first name in their favorite color and draw a picture of (1) something they like to eat (2) some-they like to do (3) something they don't like to eat. Explain that just like they learned alot about me from pictures, they can learn about each other. Tell them not to draw too well...so we can have fun guessing what it is. When finished drawing...take turns guessing what the drawings represent.

Keep the name tags out where everyone can see them and learn each other's name

SCRIBBLE IN:

(DRAW AN UGLY PICTURE) Ask them to draw the ugliest picture they can draw. Tell them that in school they try to draw the best they can...but the art here will be different than what they do in school. They will not have many instructions. They will be able to make more decisions themselves. They will be able to draw what they feel like drawing. Begin by drawing what you think is an ugly picture...
                    DRAW...SHARE
Ask them what they think makes their picture ugly. Take a vote for the ugliest picture. Most will draw what they consider an ugly person or alot of scribbles. Tell them scribbles are the way everyone begins to draw. All great artists scribble before they learn to draw. Tell them you think they will learn to have fun with scribbles again. We will have a SCRIBBLE IN and a SCRIBBLE OUT each session.

CHECK IN:
Suggest a weekly check in to share what kind of a week they had, and how they are feeling. Ask for suggestions of how quick scribble drawings could be used. (draw a feeling face each week...or a pot that is full or empty...or a thermometer that is up or down, etc.) Decide which to use each week.

B. CONTENT

INTRODUCTION:

The group will vary with the reasons for children being being in the group. Some groups may have a variety of illnesses and others may all be a form of cancer, diabetes, etc. Check the additional reading book list in the beginning of the workbook for suggestions of books to use for an introduction. I like to use books that have mainly pictures and very few words. It is quite easy to find books for this first session that show change in nature.

TODAY:
We are going to talk about the many changes that are a natural part of life.

Page 1.   CHANGE IS A NATURAL PART OF LIFE. Ask the group to think of something they could draw in these two boxes that would be the same thing...but different times of the year that would show change. (They often need a few ideas to begin the first pages)
                        DRAW...SHARE

Discuss the many changes that are natural in nature. (Trees, lakes, flowers, seasons, weather) Ask them what the world would be like without change....

Page 2.   PEOPLE CHANGE TOO! Ask them if they have seen a picture of themself as a baby...and how were they different. Ask them to draw a quick picture of how they looked then...and now.
                        DRAW...SHARE

Page 3.   CHANGE BRINGS GAINS AND LOSSES. Read.
                        DRAW...SHARE

Children often associate being a baby with being held and loved. Learning to walk and talk is a very positive change. Babies could only cry to get what they needed and hope someone would know what it was they wanted. Words are much more effective.

Page 4.   SOMEONE IN MY FAMILY HAS A SERIOUS ILLNESS. Read. (From now on, try not to put ideas in their heads. Encourage them to decide themself what they want to draw. It is their book and their story. Tell them any way they want to do it will be all right. This is not like school. There will not be many directions.)
                        DRAW...SHARE

(This may not be easy for everyone. Maybe as others share, they will recognize their own changes.) Stress that it is O.K. to have problems...and it is O.K to talk about them. Pretending everything is O.K. isn't healthy. It takes too much energy...and is tiring!

Page 5.   THIS IS A PICTURE OF MAY FAMILY...BEFORE. Read.
                        DRAW...SHARE

page 6.   THIS IS A PICTURE OF MY FAMILY...AFTER. Read.
                        DRAW...SHARE

(Changes may be recognized more after drawing than before. Drawing often reveals unconscious thoughts and feelings.) Tell them that change is part of life. It isn't always easy. We'll learn in this group healthy ways to cope with change.

MOVING ON: Have simple props for acting out baby, teen, parent, and grandparent. Object is to make the group laugh or cry. Both feelings are O.K. Choose a spot that that can be stage. As soon as one person laughs...or cries, the next person has a turn. This is an activity to involve body movement, and does not require much time.

C. ENDING

THIS WEEK: We talked alot about change and a little bit about serious illness.

NEXT WEEK We will learn some facts about illness and why people get sick.

SCRIBBLE OUT:

(SCRIBBLE PICTURE) On a scribble sheet, draw a big smile with a line across to make a bowl. Draw some lines of different colors coming out. Then use bright colors and alot of different scribbles to make flowers...make many kinds. There are all kinds of flowers. Scribbles can be beautiful! (Encourage them to color hard to get bright colors. They can experiment on the other side with more flowers.

UPS AND DOWNS:

Tell them it is important to be able to learn to share how they feel about what happens in the group. Begin by sharing what they didn't like...anything... what we did or didn't do...what someone said or did. (Respond by thanking them for sharing...no excuses or reasons.

Next, invite them to share what they did like, and again respond with a simple, "thank you for sharing that."

CREATIVE GOODBYE:

It is important to say goodbye. There are many different ways to say goodbye. Let the group decide how they would like to say goodbye. It should be something similar each time to give them the security of structure. (Some suggestions: goodbye in a foreign language each time, As a group say goodbye to each person in the group, write a goodbye poem and say it each week, taking hands and saying goodbye together, etc.)

Before the group says their goodbye, ask them how they felt about our time together. Ask them if they want to come again next week. (I believe they should be part of the group only if they want to be.)

Say: Our time is up. I've enjoyed getting to know you...and I look forward to next week. It's time to say goodbye now....

SESSION II

UNDERSTANDING SERIOUS ILLNESS p. 7-13
  Define serious and other illness
  Learn basic cause of illness
  Identify body parts effected by illness
  Assess understanding and misconceptions

A. BEGINNING

SNACK: The child that brought the snack serves it and cleans
          up afterwards. This increases self esteem and
          and decreases feelings of helplessness.

GATHERING: (CHANGING TIME CARDS) Cut out pictures of changes
          in nature and childhood changes. (seasons, water...
          ice, etc. crib, bottle, baby sitters, Parent going
          to work, school, pet loss, funeral, suitcase, house
          for sale, etc.) Let each child choose a card and
          share something about the way they felt about that
          change.

SCRIBBLE IN:
          (CHANGING PICTURE) Ask the group to think about a
          picture they would like to draw...and plan for a
          few moments how they would like it to look. Invite them
          to close their eyes and see that picture in their mind.
          Draw anything they would like...something fun and easy.
          (always use newprint for scribble in and out activity.)

          When they all have a picture pretty well started,
          say: This is going to be what I call a changing
          picture...Do you know what that is? Pass your picture
          to the person on your right. Now, add something to
          the picture in front of you. Add something that will
          make it more interesting.

          Let them draw for a few minutes...and again say:
          Stop! Pass your picture to the right. Continue this
          way allowing about a minute per picture until their
          original drawing comes back to the original drawer.

          Ask them how they feel about the finished picture...
          Do they like it or dislike it? What are they feeling?
          Is it changed from the way they imagined it would be?

          Change is like that. Everyone has different feelings
          about what has changed.

CHECK IN: Draw something on the back of the scribble sheet
          that tells something about what kind of a week they had.
                    DRAW...SHARE

B. CONTENT

LAST WEEK: We talked about the many changes that are part of life.

THIS WEEK: We are going to learn some facts about some different kinds of illnesses.

Page 7.   THIS IS A PICTURE OF THE PERSON... Read
                    DRAW...SHARE

(Does the person look well or sick...thin...in a wheel chair, in bed, standing, etc. This will be different for different kinds of illness.)

HE OR SHE GOT SICK BECAUSE.... (This can be very important. You can say, "It is hard to know why a person gets sick sometimes...but do you have any thoughts about it?"

Say, "Those are interesting thoughts. We'll learn more about what causes illness today.."

Page 8.   THE ILLNESS IS CALLED... Read (some may need help)
                    WRITE...SHARE

Suggest that sometimes children aren't told many facts about illness because adults think they can't understand or are not interested. Children CAN understand basic facts and need to know. It is O.K. to ask adults and doctors questions. There is a page at the beginning of this book with addresses to write for basic information about many diseases. Encourage children to get more information about their family illness from parents, doctor, school library, etc.

Page 9.   Invite children to learn more about general illness. Suggest they take turns reading the page. Ask for questions. Let them all repeat the terms. Children like big words.

Page 10.   Continue letting the children take turns reading. This is very basic information that children will absorb according to their age and interest level. Some will be fascinated. Some will be bored. That is O.K. Don't try to force a biology course on them. Children wonder who else will get sick...including themself. When a parent has cancer, children worry that normal aches and pains are cancer too. Education can help dissolve fears. Children fear the unknown and anticipate the worst.

Page 11.   ILLNESS MAY SHOW OUTSIDE THE BODY... Read.Discuss diseases that show on the outside.
                    DRAW...SHARE

Sometimes it is harder to accept and understand an illness that doesn't have many visible symptoms.

Page 12.   Illness always affects some part of the body. Read.
                   DRAW...SHARE

               If the facilitator is a nurse and understands the
               illnesses in the group, this can be an educating
               page. If not, it can be communication for parents
               and misconceptions can be corrected by them. Encourage
               children to learn more about the illness.

Page 13.   SOME PEOPLE WITH SERIOUS ILLNESS ARE TREATED... Read.
                   DRAW...SHARE
               (More family changes may be recognized and talked about.
               If parents are gone more, who takes care of the child's
               needs...Does the child feel lonely? What is the
               parent unable to do? If a sibling is sick, how do
               they feel about the attention they need? Separation
               is an important issue.

MOVING ON:(RELAXATION) Use a relaxation tape for children or do
               a brief progressive relaxation teaching them to breathe
               deeply, tense muscles and relax them.

C. ENDING

   THIS WEEK: We learned some important facts about illness. People
               have all kinds of feelings when there is serious
               illness in a family.

   NEXT WEEK:We will learn more about all kinds of feelings.

   SCRIBBLE OUT:
               (FRIENDLY CHASE) Families with illnesses may have
               disagreements. It isn't easy for friends to get
               along all the time either. Our scribble out today
               will require partners. Identify partners sitting
               next to each other. Partners must choose a color
               that is different. One will be the leader and
               one will be the follower. Decide who will be the
               leader. The leader begins to scribble on the
               newsprint and the follower follows the same line as
               close as possible.

               Next...change roles and repeat exercise on other side
               of paper.

               Ask: Which role did you like best? Follower or
               leader? We are all different. Some prefer leading
               and some prefer following. What do you have in your
               family...leaders...followers...or both? What happens
               if everyone wants to lead?

   UPS AND DOWNS:
               What troubled you today...what did you like?

   CREATIVE GOODBYE:
               As group decided, but it is important for group
               members to say goodbye to each other...not just
               the facilitator.

SESSION III

FEELINGS ABOUT FAMILY CHANGE p. 14-19
Recognize and name feelings
Learn that feelings are all O.K.
Discover defense masks
Identify feelings about family changes

A. BEGINNING

SNACK: As before.

GATHERING: (STUFFED FEELINGS) Copy the list of feelings on page 15 in the workbook. Cut them into individual pieces of paper and "stuff" into a small jar with a cover. Spin the jar and the person it points to when it stops picks a paper...and shares a time when they felt that feeling. They have the right to pass if they choose.

SCRIBBLE IN:

(FEELING COLORS) Feelings can be expressed with colors. Try different colors and decide which color you like best to show anger, fear, sadness, and joy.

Next...decide what kind of lines express those same feelings best. There is no right way. People will all choose different lines and colors...but some may be similar.

CHECK IN: As decided by the group.

B. CONTENT

LAST WEEK: We talked about different ways serious illness brings family changes.

TODAY: We'll learn about feelings that are part of change. (Read pages from an appropriate book.)

Page 14. GRIEF SHEET. Invite children to color page with appropriate colors. Ask them what colors they think would be good for "shock". Suggest they scribble a variety of colors for confused feelings. Pink or green might be a good color for growth and healing. (Younger children may not understand alot of this but they can learn that GRIEF is the name for the many feelings that come with change. They can also learn that feelings come and go.

Page 15. THERE MAY BE MANY FEELINGS. (Children can do this very quickly and can learn the names of feelings they see on other's faces.) DRAW...SHARE

Page 16. SOMETIMES PEOPLE PUT ON A MASK... Read. Invite children to draw three feelings that are difficult for them to show...and sometimes hide.
SHARE

(It is important for them to know that others do this also...so you can't be sure of what a person is feeling by the look on their face.

Page 17.   FEELINGS ARE SOMETHING YOU FEEL IN YOUR BODY. Begin with anger because it is usually the easiest to identify. Invite children to close their eyes and think of a time when they were very angry at someone..or something. Someone may have taken something away from you or were mean to you. Where do you feel anger in your body when you think about that time? Use a red crayon and scribble it in at that place on the picture of the body...a little or alot, whatever you feel.

Next...use blue and think of a time when you felt very sad. Close your eyes and decide where you feel sadness in your body...and color that place blue.

Remember a time when you were really scared. Maybe you had a nightmare or maybe it was something else. Close your eyes and decide where you feel that feeling and color it in.

Continue with the other colors. You may need to make suggestions of when they might have felt those feelings. This is an important page and time is required.

(Assessment: With children, I use this mainly to emphasize the need to express feelings to avoid aches and pains in those areas. However, lack of colors suggest repressed feelings. They need to learn that feelings are all O.K. Colors mixed up and scribbled all over suggest confusion or being overwhelmed by many feelings. Coloring very neatly suggests controlling feelings. Parts of the body colored like a patch-work quilt suggest they are unable to identify where they feel feelings.

Page 18.   IF FEELINGS ARE STUFFED INSIDE... Read directions and invite them to color any areas they get aches and pains.
                        DRAW...SHARE

Look back at page 13 and see if anger and fear or other feelings are felt in the same places they get aches and pains. Headaches, stomach aches and back aches are often the result of stuffed feelings.

Hands , feet, and the mouth are natural energy zones for feelings. That is why young children bite, hit and kick. It is important to substitute acceptable behaviors that use the same zones.

Page 19.   WHAT DO PEOPLE IN YOUR FAMILY DO WHEN THEY FEEL...
                Read the lines at the bottom of the page and remind
                children that people have different feelings and have
                different ways of letting feelings out.
                         DRAW...SHARE

MOVING ON:(FOLLOW THE FEELING PERSON) Invite children to stand
                and stretch. Play a game like "follow the leader".
                Choose an active child to be the first leader and line
                others behind. Invite the leader to act out a feeling
                using both face and body. The others follow and do
                the same thing for a few minutes. The leader goes
                to the end of the line and a new leader begins.

C. ENDING

THIS WEEK: We learned to recognize and name many different feelings
                that might be part of experiencing family changes. We
                learned that all feelings are O.K.

NEXT WEEK: We will learn more about feelings and how to cope with
                them.

SCRIBBLE OUT:
                (TEAR UP) Draw something scary like a nightmare
                or a monster. Draw something with the hand you
                usually don't write with. Draw something very
                powerful to destroy the scary thing. Tear the
                picture into small pieces.

UPS AND DOWNS:
                What made you feel down today...and up today?

CREATIVE GOODBYE:
                As group has decided.

SESSION IV

DRAWING OUT DIFFICULT FEELINGS p. 20-24
Recognize effect of feelings on behavior
See family pattern of expressing feelings
Identify personal difficult feelings
Learn healthy ways to express feelings

A. BEGINNING

SNACK: As before

GATHERING: (ADD-A-LONG FEELING) Begin with...MY FRIEND WAS
FEELING_____ BECAUSE_____. The child to
the right of you repeats what you said and adds...
AND THE DAY BEFORE SHE WAS FEELING_____ BECAUSE__
___. Each next person repeats and adds. Continue
until someone mixes up and drops out. The last
person left wins.

SCRIBBLE IN:
(GUESSING FEELINGS) Draw a difficult feeling you
felt last week and something about why you felt it.
The person who guesses correctly shows their picture
next.

CHECK IN: As group decided.

B. CONTENT

LAST WEEK: We learned to recognize and name many kinds of
feelings. we learned that if we stuff too many
feelings too long, they often cause aches and
pains.

TODAY: We are going to talk about some of the more difficult
feelings and learn healthy ways to let feelings out.

Read appropriate pages of book if desired.

Page 20.   I FEEL ANGRY WHEN... Read. Ask children to draw
a picture of the things or things that they get
angry about most often. You might ask them if
anything about the illness that makes them angry.
DRAW...SHARE

Emphasize that anger is a natural feeling at times.
Sometimes we try to hide anger with different words
like hurt...disappointed...upset...cranky. It is
O.K. to feel angry.

Page 21.   WHEN I FEEL ANGRY, I...Ask them what they DO when
            they feel angry. Suggest they think about a time
            they felt very angry at siblings, parents, teachers
            or friends...and remember what they did.
                          DRAW...SHARE

            Read sentence on bottom of page. Ask children to
            look at their page and cross out things that are not
            O.K. This can be done as a group decision or a
            personal decision.

Page 22.   SOMETIMES I FEEL FRIGHTENED...Read. Tell them
            everyone feels frightened at times. Ask them if
            there is anything about the illness that they
            have fears about. If not, think about what they
            do sometimes feel frightened about.
                          DRAW...SHARE

            WHEN I FEEL FRIGHTENED, I... Read. DRAW...SHARE

            Some people run away when they are afraid. Some
            people freeze and can't move. What do you do?
            Many people try to hide their fears...is that
            O.K.? (Facilitator can share childhood fears
            and how they have changed) Discuss nightmares
            and bad dreams. Do they come after watching
            T.V. or movies? Suggest they make good T.V.
            choices.

Page 23.   THERE ARE TIMES I FEEL HELPLESS. Read. Suggest
            that when someone has a serious illness, there
            must be times that everyone else in the family
            feels helpless because there are things they just
            can't do. Ask them to think about what makes
            them feel helpless.
                          DRAW...SHARE

            (Children often feel helpless when they can't do
            something to make parents feel happy...or they
            can't make the person well.) Remind them that
            there will be times that people have problems.
            Children don't cause them...and they can't fix
            them.

Page 24.   OTHER TIMES I JUST FEEL SAD. Read. Ask if there
            are times or places that they feel especially
            sad about the illness.
                          DRAW...SHARE

            Children often associate crying with babies because
            babies cry to get their needs met until they learn
            words. When a person can talk they are encouraged
            to use words to ask for what they need. Crying
            to let sadness out is O.K. for every age.

MOVING ON:(DEFENSE MASKS) Have three masks showing the
feelings of being happy, sad and angry. Pick
two volunteers. Have one act one feeling wearing
a mask...but keeping a different feeling inside.
The other will respond to the actor.

When finished, others may try. Ask them afterwards
how it felt to be the actor...and how it felt to
be the other person. (Masks or defensive feelings
are like walls. They keep you from being close
to the other person. It takes alot of energy to
act differently than you feel.)

C. ENDING

THIS WEEK: We talked about difficult feelings and learned
O.K. ways to let feelings out.

NEXT WEEK:We will talk about living with changes from illness
and learn how to take good care of ourselves.

SCRIBBLE OUT:
(SCRIBBLE OUT ANGER) Think about someone you
often feel angry at. (This is often a sibling)
Draw a symbol or stick person like that person
with a red crayon. Think about your anger...
put it on the paper by scribbling out
the symbol. Scribble really hard until the anger
is all gone. Next, scrunch the paper into a ball
and throw it at a blank wall. Finally throw it
in a waste basket and try to forget about it.
(Children love this. It is a healthy release
of anger. They may need to be reminded that this
doesn't hurt the person.)

UPS AND DOWNS:
What made you feel down today...and up today?

CREATIVE GOODBYE:
Thank them for sharing and working hard. Say
goodbye in the usual way.

SESSION V

LIVING WELL WITH ILLNESS p. 25-30
Assess family coping skills
Recognize personal needs
Identify support resources
Learn healthy coping skills

A. BEGINNING

SNACK: As before

GATHERING: Share a favorite memory...something they remember about
a time when they were happy and having fun.

SCRIBBLE IN:
On a sheet of newsprint, have children write the initials
of their first and last name. Add colors and lines to
turn the initials into a picture. They can turn the
paper any direction that works best.

CHECK IN: As group decided

B. CONTENT

LAST WEEK: We talked about difficult feelings and learned O.K.
ways to let them out.

TODAY: We will talk about living with changes from illness and
learn how to take good care of ourselves.
(Read appropriate pages from book if desired.)

Page 25.   EVERYONE IN A FAMILY IS AFFECTED BY SERIOUS ILLNESS.
Read. Discuss. (Young children may not understand
the concepts. Suggest that a person with an illness
needs alot of attention. Others may need to find
ways that work best for them to get the attention
they need, also. Do people in your family do any
of these things?

                    DRAW...SHARE
Ask them how these ways could be a problem if they
become a habit. This happens when the illness lasts
a long time. (Perfect...perfectionism; problem...
self destructive behavior; forgotten...low expectations
and passive; sick...hypochondriac; fixer...co-dependent;
clown...lonely, not taken seriously.)

Page 26.   ILLNESS BRINGS STRESS... Take turns reading sentences.
Suggest they check the things they are already doing.
Put a star on the things they need to do.

Page 27.   MANY PEOPLE CARE ABOUT ME...   Read   Invite them to
list the people who are important to them. Next, place
the number in the circle. This is a good time to
explain relationships. Some people are close to you
like parents and family. Others are not as close to
you...you don't see them as often...but they are still
important to you. Other grown ups in schools, churches
and other places care alot about children also. (They
need to know that many people care about them to feel
more secure.)
                    DRAW...SHARE

Ask them who they can talk to about problems. They
can mark that person with a star.

This is a good time to talk about relationships. Caring,
sharing and working together makes good friendships.
Talk about treating siblings with respect. Encourage
them to practice group rules at home as well as in group.

Page 28.   MY FAMILY IS LEARNING TO LIVE WELL TOGETHER. Read.
Draw or write the things you do in your family.
                    SHARE

These are all important ways to keep healthy. There
are many disadvantages to illness in the family. One
advantage is that everyone can learn to appreciate
good health and learn healthy living skills.

Page 29.   THERE MAY BE TIMES WHEN SPECIAL PEOPLE ARE GONE
OR TOO BUSY... Read.
                    DRAW...SHARE

(One reason pets are important to children is that they
are always there. Pets, dolls, stuffed animals, etc.
are also very good listeners to tell troubles to. It
is important to have something.)

Page 30.   MANY PEOPLE HAVE GOD, A GUARDIAN ANGEL OR.   Read.
                    DRAW...SHARE

Younger children often give this power to their parents.
Children who pray to God to make someone well may be
angry when that doesn't happen and lose faith. Respect
the different beliefs.

MOVING ON: (TALK AND TOSS) Hold a ball of yarn and explain rules. Only the person holding the yarn can talk. Toss the ball to a child and share one thing they like about themself...and then toss the ball across the group to someone else for their turn. Continue. A web will be be formed. Talk about relationships and connections. Talk about the need for independence and inter-dependence. Cut the yarn and give each child pieces to take home to make a friendship bracelet...or this can be done in group if there is time.

C. ENDING

THIS WEEK: We talked about ways we live happier with family changes. You are learning to share feelings in this group and you can do that with your parents also.

NEXT WEEK We will talk more about personal strengths and our relationships with others. It will be our last week for these groups and we will have a celebration. (Some groups may decide to invite a parent to the celebration. If so plan accordingly.)

UPS AND DOWNS:
What do you feel down about...what do you feel good about?

SCRIBBLE OUT:
Play a peppy tape in the tape player you brought (opera is good for a variety of feelings). Invite children to use colors and lines to show what they hear in the music. Begin with the dominant hand. After a few minutes suggest they try the other hand. Compare. (the dominant hand is usually less free)

CREATIVE GOODBYE:
Thank them and say goodbye as planned.

SESSION VI

FEELING GOOD ABOUT ME p. 31-36
   Learn that play is the work of childhood
   Increase feelings of self-esteem
   Celebrate family strengths
   Express hopes and dreams

A. BEGINNING

SNACK: Save snack for ending celebration. (cup cakes preferred)

GATHERING: (Before group begins, print these words on a piece of construction paper: PRETTY, HANDSOME, HONEST, STRONG, FRIENDLY, FUNNY, HELPFUL, CARING, NICE, NEAT, COOL, FOXY, GREAT.) Show sheet to children and ask them which 6 (or whatever the number in the group) they consider the most important. Give each child one of the chosen words to copy on colored slips of paper (about1"x2" the number in the group) and save for the moving on activity.

SCRIBBLE IN:
(ROAD MAP OF LIFE) On a sheet of newsprint, draw the ups and downs of your life so far...the road blocks, the bumpy times, the dead ends, the high times, the the bridges. Next, think ahead and draw a road map for your future. What good things do you hope for? Will there still be bumpy times?

CHECK IN: As decided by the group. Also ask how they feel about this being the last session.

B. CONTENT

LAST WEEK: We talked about healthy ways we could live well together. in our family.

TODAY: We will talk more about ourselves and things we feel good about.

Page 31.   SOMETIMES I DON'T LIKE TO THINK ABOUT THE ILLNESS. Read. Ask them if they think it is O.K. to feel happy and have fun when someone else is sick? Of course it is! Ask them to think about who they have fun with and what they like to do.   DRAW...SHARE

(Children often need permission to be happy when adults have so much sadness about serious illness.

Page 32.   THERE ARE TIMES I HAVE EXTRA WORK...Read.
                   DRAW...SHARE

(Some children may seem to have more responsibilites than is age appropriate. Others may not have any expectations or opportunities to be helpful.

Page 33.   MY FAMILY IS SPECIAL... Read. Ask them to think about
            something special about each member of their family...
            and then decide how they can put that into a picture.
            Some words are O.K.
                        DRAW...SHARE

            (Encourage them to find something good about each
            person, and something about the sick person besides
            being sick. Children are often embarrassed about
            obvious signs of the illness like baldness, wheelchairs,
            oxygen tubes, etc. They don't like to be different.
            It helps them to talk about it in a group.)

Page 34.   I AM SPECIAL TOO... Read. (Most children are able
            to think of several things they are good at. Those
            who can't have poor self esteem and need help in
            recognizing their abilities and special gifts.)
                        DRAW...SHARE

Page 35.   UNEXPECTED BLESSINGS MAY COME... Children are often
            more positive than adults and think of gains as well
            as losses that come with change. (Appreciation,
            compassion, time, education, love, learning a variety
            of things. Read.
                        DRAW...SHARE

Page 36.   IT'S ALWAYS GOOD TO HAVE HOPES AND DREAMS... Read.
                        DRAW...SHARE

            (Children may wish for a cure, a special time, more
            time, less pain. Everyone has special wishes.)

MOVING ON: (POSITIVE OBSTACLES) Arrange chairs for a simple
            obstacle course to crawl under or climb over. Give
            children a spot to stand and the positive statement
            slips they made earlier in this session. Take turns
            going around the course, stopping to recieve a slip
            from each child as they say, "You are...or are going
            to be (which ever they choose to say)_____.
            The facilitator takes the place of the child going
            around and hands out their slip while they are gone.
            The children keep their slips to paste on a sheet with
            the group photo.

CELEBRATION:
            Take a group picture using a polaroid camera (or a
            regular camera the week before and get prints) Have
            an 8x10 sheet of colored construction paper for the
            children to glue the picture and the positive words on.
            Let each child sign their name to the sheet so they
            will have something to remember their time together.

C. ENDING

THIS WEEK: We have had our 6th and last session. You have worked really hard and I have enjoyed our time together. I feel good about the things you have learned.

SCRIBBLE OUT:

(GROUP MURAL) Before the session begins, draw the grief "wave" from page 8 in the workbook with a black marker on a white piece of butcher paper about 10 ft. long. Tape to a wall. Invite children to decorate the mural with different feelings of grief in appropriate places and appropriate colors and pictures. Decorate as they wish. Suggest they finish by writing O.K. in empty spaces to remind them that all feelings are O.K.

Ask children for permission to keep the mural as a memory of the group and something you might be able to use to teach others about children's grief.

UPS AND DOWNS:

As usual, but allow time for them to express feelings about the group ending. Some may have some sadness or anger. They may choose to have a reunion some time.

CREATIVE GOODBYE:

Suggest a final review of what they have learned together:
Change is a natural part of life.
Serious illness creates change and losses.
Loss creates many feelings of grief.
Feelings need to be expressed in healthy ways.
Difficult times bring opportunities for learning.
You are important and many people care about you.

Tell them their book will be a reminder of their time here and the things they learned. Encourage them to share the book with their parents because they can learn from it too.

Thank them for being part of the group and for the things you have learned from them. Wish them well and ask them if they would like to say goodbye in a special way. (a group hug is great if they want to. This is another ending for them.)

Curriculum: When Mom and Dad Separate

This book was designed to teach children some concepts about divorce and to recognize and express feelings of grief from family change, to encourage open communication and to help adults discover unhealthy misconceptions children may have. The concepts and following objectives are included in the text and may be stressed by additional reading from the books suggested for children.

SUPPLIES BOX   (BRING WEEKLY)

```
1   WORKBOOK per child
1   BOX OF 8 CRAYONS  per child
12  SHEETS 8x10 NEWSPRINT per child (scribble sheets)
1   8x10 FIRM WHITE PAPER per child (name tags)
1   8x10 COLORED CONSTRUCTION PAPER (for group rules)
    SMALL BOXES OF COLORED PENCILS ( 10-12 year olds )
    PAPER TOWELS (for spills)
    SCISSORS
    BOX OF KLEENEX
    EXTRA SNACK & PACKAGE OF LEMONADE (in case a child forgets)
    EXTRA CUPS AND NAPKINS
```

ADDITIONAL

```
WEEK I    SNACK AND BEVERAGE FOR GROUP
          CUPS AND NAPKINS
          FACILITATOR PICTURES FOR INTRODUCTION
          PROPS FOR AGE CHANGE INTERESTS (rattle, telephone,
          newspaper, book. hats, wigs, glasses, etc.)
          BOOK FROM LIST FOR INTRODUCTION (optional)


WEEK 2.   CHANGE CARDS WITH NATURE AND PEOPLE PICTURES
          TAPE PLAYER AND RELAXATION TAPE (optional)


WEEK 3.   JAR WITH COVER
          SLIPS OF PAPER WITH FEELINGS WRITTEN ON


WEEK 4.   DEFENSE MASKS (cut from paper or paper plates with binder)
```

```
WEEK 5.   BALL OF COLORED YARN (to toss and braid friendship bracelet)
          TAPE PLAYER AND OPERA OR LIVELY MUSIC TAPE
          CAMERA AND FILM (if polaroid isn't available next week)


WEEK 6.   1  SHEET OF CONSTRUCTION PAPER WITH 13 WORDS WRITTEN
          6  PIECES 2"x3" COLORED PAPER per child
          1  8"X10" SHEET COLORED CONSTRUCTION PAPER per child
          2  GLUE STICKS
          1  SHEET WHITE MEAT WRAP PAPER ABOUT 24"x8' (mural)
             POLAROID CAMERA OR PRINTS FROM LAST WEEK
             MASKING TAPE (to put mural up)
```

WHEN MOM AND DAD SEPARATE

SESSION I

CHANGE IS PART OF LIFE p.1-4
- See change as a natural part of growth
- Discuss personal change
- Identify ways of coping with change
- Discuss changes related to divorce

A. BEGINNING

SNACK: Provide a snack yourself the first session, or ask someone to bring a simple treat and juice. Have parents sign up to have child bring and serve something for the remaining sessions. Invite the child to serve...it builds self-esteem.

INTRODUCTION:

Introduce yourself. I do this with about six pictures of myself as a child in my original family, pictures in high school and my first wedding. I share that my first husband died and I raised my three boys alone for six years before I married again. I share the picture of my second wedding and our 6 teenagers. They are a wild looking bunch. I share that my new husband was divorced and his wife was unable to take care of her children so they lived with us. Finally I share a recent picture of our family at recent youngest child's wedding...and comment on the many changes in my life...and in the children's. The picture shows what fine young adults they all are now. The children seem to love this and bond and develop trust in me more quickly.

Ask them if they know why they are here and how they felt about coming. Ask for honest feelings. Ask them if they know what a grief support group is. After they share their ideas, explain that grief is the word for the many feelings that come with change. This group is a place where they can learn about those feelings and can talk about how they really feel. Everyone is here because their parents have separated or divorced.

RULES: Let the group discuss what rules they would like to have. List on construction paper and keep handy to remind them when needed. (see suggestions for rules in earlier section)

GATHERING:

(NAME TAG) Fold 9x12 paper lengthwise. Invite child to print first name in their favorite color and draw a picture of (1) something they like to eat (2) some-they like to do (3) something they don't like to eat. Explain that just like they learned alot about me from pictures, they can learn about each other.
Tell them not to draw too well...so we can have fun guessing what it is. When finished drawing...take turns guessing what the drawings represent.

Keep the name tags out where everyone can see them and learn each other's name

SCRIBBLE IN:

(DRAW AN UGLY PICTURE) Ask them to draw the ugliest picture they can draw. Tell them that in school they try to draw the best they can...but the art here will be different than what they do in school. They will not have many instructions. They will be able to make more decisions themselves. They will be able to draw what they feel like drawing. Begin by drawing what you think is an ugly picture...
                    DRAW...SHARE
Ask them what they think makes their picture ugly. Take a vote for the ugliest picture. Most will draw what they consider an ugly person or alot of scribbles. Tell them scribbles are the way everyone begins to draw. All great artists scribble before they learn to draw. Tell them you think they will learn to have fun with scribbles again. We will have a SCRIBBLE IN and a SCRIBBLE OUT each session.

CHECK IN:

Suggest a weekly check in to share what kind of a week they had, and how they are feeling. Ask for suggestions of how quick scribble drawings could be used. (draw a feeling face each week...or a pot that is full or empty...or a thermometer that is up or down, etc.) Decide which to use each week.

B. CONTENT

INTRODUCTION:

DINOSAURS DIVORCE by Laurene and Marc Brown is suggested for an introduction each week. Read a couple of pages that are appropriate for the weekly objectives. Children love the cartoon drawings. The dinosaurs seem able to tell important concepts with a little less personal identification and pain. It holds the attention of children who may be tired of hearing about divorce! Other good books are listed in the workbook. Group leaders often prefer to use more time with the suggested activities when time is limited.

TODAY:

We are going to talk about the many changes that are a natural part of life.

Page 1.   CHANGE IS PART OF LIFE. Ask the changes in nature
           the simple drawings represent. Invite them to draw
           a bigger picture of one of these changes or another
           change they can think of that is part of nature.
           (Suggestions are made only in the beginning of the
           book to help them get started.)
                      DRAW...SHARE
           Discuss how the world would be if there were no
           changes.

Page 2.   PEOPLE CHANGE TOO. Invite them to draw a picture
           of how they looked as a baby...now...and how
           they think they will look when they are very old.
           Encourage them to draw quickly.
                      DRAW...SHARE
           Discuss life changes that are part of growing...
           appearance...interests...and how they feel about
           changing. Change is easier for some people than
           others. Some see change as a challenge. SOme
           resist change and have a harder time coping. Some
           changes are big...some are small.

Page 3.   FAMILIES CHANGE. (From now on have the children
           in the group take turns reading the words on the
           page...and then draw the picture that comes into
           their mind when they hear the words. No more
           suggestions of what to draw.) Tell them it is their
           book and whatever they want to draw is O.K. If
           they want to skip a page, that is O.K. too. It will
           be different than school. There will not be many
           directions. There will not be alot of time to
           draw...they can add more details later if they
           like. They will be drawing pictures to tell their
           own story. Everyone's book will be a little bit
           different. Differences are O.K.
                      DRAW...SHARE
           Share pictures. Ask who would like to begin. They
           often draw two houses...or a picture of one parent
           moving out. Encourage discussion about how they
           learned about the separation...and if it was a
           surprise. They may or may not have much to share
           this first session. Follow their lead.

Page 4.   THERE MAY BE MANY CHANGES. READ. ASK how their
           life has changed and invite them to put that into
           a picture...or pictures.
                      DRAW...SHARE
           (Children need to recognize what has changed in
           their life before they can grieve losses. This is
           not always easy. They may have and need denial.)
           Read line at page bottom.

MOVING ON: Have simple props for acting out baby, teen, parent,
           and grandparent. Object is to make the group laugh
           or cry. Both feelings are O.K. Choose a spot that
           that can be a stage. As soon as one person laughs...or
           cries, the next person has a turn. This is an
           activity to involve body movement, and does not
           require much time.

C. ENDING

THIS WEEK: We talked alot about change and a little bit about divorce.

NEXT WEEK We'll talk about marriage and divorce and family changes.

SCRIBBLE OUT:

(SCRIBBLE PICTURE) On a scribble sheet, draw a big smile with a line across to make a bowl. Draw some lines of different colors coming out. Then use bright colors and alot of different scribbles to make flowers...make many kinds. There are all kinds of flowers. Scribbles can be beautiful! (Encourage them to color hard to get bright colors. They can experiment on the other side with more flowers.

UPS AND DOWNS:

Tell them it is important to be able to learn to share how they feel about what happens in the group. Begin by sharing what they didn't like...anything... what we did or didn't do...what someone said or did. (Respond by thanking them for sharing...no excuses or reasons.

Next, invite them to share what they did like, and again respond with a simple, "thank you for sharing that."

CREATIVE GOODBYE:

It is important to say goodbye. There are many different ways to say goodbye. Let the group decide how they would like to say goodbye. It should be something similar each time to give them the security of structure. (Some suggestions: goodbye in a foreign language each time, As a group say goodbye to each person in the group, write a goodbye poem and say it each week, taking hands and saying goodbye together, etc.)

Before the group says their goodbye, ask them how they felt about our time together. Ask them if they want to come again next week. (I believe they should be part of the group only if they want to be.)

Say: Our time is up. I've enjoyed getting to know you...and I look forward to next week. It's time to say goodbye now....

SESSION II

UNDERSTANDING DIVORCE p.5-9
Learn concepts of marriage and divorce
Assess placement of blame
Identify misconceptions
Recognize personal changes

A. BEGINNING

SNACK: The child that brought the snack serves it and cleans up afterwards. This increases self esteem and and decreases feelings of helplessness.

GATHERING: (CHANGING TIME CARDS) Cut out pictures of changes in nature and childhood changes. (seasons, water... ice, etc. crib, bottle, baby sitters, Parent going to work, school, pet loss, funeral, suitcase, house for sale, etc.) Let each child choose a card and share something about the way they felt about that change.

SCRIBBLE IN:

(CHANGING PICTURE) Ask the group to think about a picture they would like to draw...and plan for a few moments how would like it to look. Invite them to close their eyes and see that picture in their mind. Draw anything they would like...something fun and easy. (always use newprint for scribble in and out activity.)

When they all have a picture pretty well started, say: This is going to be what I call a changing picture...Do you know what that is? Pass your picture to the person on your right. Now, add something to the picture in front of you. Add something that will make it more interesting.

Let them draw for a few minutes...and again say: Stop! Pass your picture to the right. Continue this way allowing about a minute per picture until their original drawing comes back to the original drawer.

Ask them how they feel about the finished picture... Do they like it or dislike it? What are they feeling? Is it changed from the way they imagined it would be?

Change is like that. Everyone has different feelings about what has changed.

CHECK IN: Draw something on the back of the scribble sheet that tells something about what kind of a week they had.
DRAW...SHARE

B. CONTENT

LAST WEEK: We talked about the many changes that are part of life.

THIS WEEK: We will talk about family changes that are often a part of separation or divorce.

Page 5.   MARRIAGE. Invite them to draw a picture of a marriage...and write some reasons they think people get married.
DRAW...SHARE

(Most children draw a bride and groom with smiles.) Using a different color write reasons for getting married that others have mentioned. (lonely...want a baby...need money...want to leave home...ride to work...want to be together, etc.) Check some of the reasons they think are better than others. (It is important for children to know that people often get married for more reasons than love.) It is O.K. for them to ask their parents why they got married. Parent's have the right to answer or not.

Page 6.   MARRIAGE IS...Let the children take turns reading the sentences. They can check the ones that have happened in their family IF they want to. They can also cross out the ones they don't agree with.

Discuss LOVE. Who...what...do they love? Mom, Dad, pet, peanut butter, sports, grandparents, etc. There are different kinds of love. (Romantic, conditional, unconditional, friendship, etc. Parent's love for a child is different than their love for their spouse.

Page 7.   DIVORCE. Draw. (Children often draw a picture of two people before a judge, similar to the wedding picture.) Invite them to write reasons they think people get divorced using one color. Add other's reasons in a different color during discussion.
SHARE

(It is important for children to learn there are more reasons for a divorce than not loving each other...like different ideas about money, sex, work, politics, people, friends, places to go, children, etc.)

Page 8.   DIVORCE IS...Let children take turns reading. They may check sentences they agree with, and cross out ones they don't agree with. This page helps clarify misconceptions about reasons for divorce.

Page 9.   CHILDREN'S LIVES CHANGE... (It is important to recognize what has been lost in order to grieve.) Suggest to them that there may be BIG losses and LITTLE losses. Some are easier to see than others. Invite them to draw their most difficult loss. (They may use some words if needed.)
DRAW ...SHARE

MOVING ON: (RELAXATION) Use a relaxation tape for children or do a brief progressive relaxation teaching them to breathe deeply, tense muscles and relax them.

C. ENDING

THIS WEEK: We talked about marriage and divorce and learned more about each other. Everyone has lots of feelings about separation and divorce.

NEXT WEEK: We will learn more about all kinds of feelings.

SCRIBBLE OUT:

(FRIENDLY CHASE) It isn't easy for two people to live together. It isn't easy for friends to get along all the time either. Our scribble out today will require partners. Identify partners sitting next to each other. Partners must choose a color that is different. One will be the leader and one will be the follower. Decide who will be the leader. The leader begins to scribble on the newsprint and the follower follows the same line as close as possible.

Next...change roles and repeat exercise on other side of paper.

Ask: Which role did you like best? Follower or leader? We are all different. Some prefer leading and some prefer following. What do you have in your family...leaders...followers...or both? What happens if everyone wants to lead?

UPS AND DOWNS:

What troubled you today...what did you like?

CREATIVE GOODBYE:

As group decided, but it is important for group members to say goodbye to each other...not just the facilitator.

SESSION III

FEELINGS ABOUT DIVORCE p.10-15
Recognize grief as a reaction to loss
Accept all feelings as o.k.
Recognize/name basic feelings
Identify difficult feelings

A. BEGINNING

SNACK: As before.

GATHERING: (STUFFED FEELINGS) Copy the list of feelings on page 15 in the workbook. Cut them into individual pieces of paper and "stuff" into a small jar with a cover. Spin the jar and the person it points to when it stops picks a paper...and shares a time when they felt that feeling. They have the right to pass if they choose.

SCRIBBLE IN:

(FEELING COLORS) Feelings can be expressed with colors. Try different colors and decide which color you like best to show anger, fear, sadness, and joy.

Next...decide what kind of lines express those same feelings best. There is no right way. People will all choose different lines and colors...but some may be similar.

CHECK IN: As decided by the group.

B. CONTENT

LAST WEEK: We talked about the ways separation and divorce creates family changes.

TODAY: We'll learn about feelings that are part of change. (Read pages from an appropriate book.)

Page 10. GRIEF SHEET. Invite children to color page with appropriate colors. As them what colors they think would be good for "shock". Suggest they scribble a variety of colors for confused feelings. Pink or green might be a good color for growth and healing. (Younger children may not understand alot of this but they can learn that GRIEF is the name for the many feelings that come with change. They can also learn that feelings come and go.

Page 11. FEELINGS ARE ALL O.K. Draw. (Children can do this very quickly and can learn the names of feelings they see on other's faces.)

Page 12. SOMETIMES PEOPLE PUT ON A MASK... Read. Invite children to draw three feelings that are difficult for them to show...and sometimes hide.

SHARE

(It is important for them to know that others do
this also...so you can't be sure of what a person
is feeling by the look on their face.

Page 13.   FEELINGS ARE SOMETHING YOU FEEL IN YOUR BODY.
Begin with anger because it is usually the easiest
to identify. Invite children to close their eyes
and think of a time when they were very angry at
someone..or something. Someone may have taken
something away from you or were mean to you. Where
do you feel anger in your body when you think about
that time? Use a red crayon and scribble it in at
that place on the picture of the body...a little
or alot, whatever you feel.

Next...use blue and think of a time when you felt
very sad. Close your eyes and decide where you
feel sadness in your body...and color that place
blue.

Remember a time when you were really scared. Maybe
you had a nightmare or maybe it was something else.
Close your eyes and decide where you feel that
feeling and color it in.

Continue with the other colors. You may need to
make suggestions of when they might have felt those
feelings. This is an important page and time is
required.

(Assessment: With children, I use this mainly to
emphasize the need to express feelings to avoid
aches and pains in those areas. However, lack of
colors suggest repressed feelings. They need to
learn that feelings are all O.K. Colors mixed up
and scribbled all over suggest confusion or being
overwhelmed by many feelings. Coloring very neatly
suggest controlling feelings. Parts of the body
colored like a patch-work quilt suggest they are
unable to identify where they feel feelings.

Page 14.   IF FEELINGS ARE STUFFED INSIDE... Read directions
and invite them to color any areas they get aches
and pains.
                        DRAW...SHARE

Look back at page 13 and see if anger and fear or
other feelings are felt in the same places they get
aches and pains. Headaches, stomach aches and back
aches are often the result of stuffed feelings.

Hands , feet, and the mouth are natural energy zones
for feelings. That is why young children bite, hit
and kick. It is important to substitute acceptable
behaviors that use the same zones.

Page 15.   CHECK THE FEELINGS... Follow directions. Explain
                any words they do not understand when finished.

                (Note feelings which are triple checked. Note
                feelings not checked and which may suggest poor
                self esteem. Stress that all feelings are O.K.)

MOVING ON: (FOLLOW THE FEELING PERSON) Invite children to stand
and stretch. Play a game like "follow the leader".
Choose an active child to be the first leader and line
others behind. Invite the leader to act out a feeling
using both face and body. The others follow and do
the same thing for a few minutes. The leader goes
to the end of the line and a new leader begins.

C. ENDING

THIS WEEK: We learned to recognize and name many different feelings
that might be part of experiencing a terrible event. We
learned that all feelings are O.K.

NEXT WEEK: We will learn more about feelings and how to cope with
them.

SCRIBBLE OUT:
(DRAWING WITH THE NON DOMINANT HAND) Draw a picture
using the hand you don't usually write with. It can
be a picture that is timely for this time of the
year...or it could be about a time when you had a
strong feeling.

UPS AND DOWNS:
What made you feel down today...and up today?

CREATIVE GOODBYE:
As group has decided.

SESSION IV

EXPRESSING FEELINGS p. 16-21
Identify fears and worries
Recognize unhealthy misconceptions
Learn healthy ways to express feelings
Begin sharing feelings

A. BEGINNING

SNACK: As before

GATHERING: (ADD-A-LONG FEELING) Begin with...MY FRIEND WAS FEELING_____ BECAUSE_____. The child to the right of you repeats what you said and adds... AND THE DAY BEFORE SHE WAS FEELING_____ BECAUSE___. Each next person repeats and adds. Continue until someone mixes up and drops out. The last person left wins.

SCRIBBLE IN: (GUESSING FEELINGS) Draw a difficult feeling you felt last week and something about why you felt it. The person who guesses correctly shows their picture next.

CHECK IN: As group decided.

B. CONTENT

LAST WEEK: We learned to recognize and name many kinds of feelings. we learned that if we stuff too many feelings too long, they often cause aches and pains.

TODAY: We are going to talk about some of the more difficult feelings and learn healthy ways to let feelings out.

Read appropriate pages of book if desired.

Page 16 EVERYONE FEELS ANGRY...Read and draw or use some words. (Older children often use more words than younger children.)

Stress words at the bottom of the page and follow directions drawing an X through ways that are not O.K. and circling ways that are O.K.

Page 18. YOU CAN LEARN TO LET ANGER OUT... Take turns reading. Invite them to make a check by the number if it is something they already do...and a star by a number if it is something they will try.

Remind them of the three energy zones (mouth, feet and hands) and discuss the ways some of these ideas use those zones.

Page 19.   CHILDREN MAY FEEL VERY SAD...Suggest that many...
            but not all...children feel sadness about a
            divorce.   DRAW...SHARE

            (Younger children are usually bonded more to Mom
            and have more sadness if she is the one that moves
            out. It is important to give permission to be sad
            or not be sad. Children need permission to cry.
            They often associate crying with babies. It is
            helpful to remind them that babies cry to get their
            needs met until they learn words. It's better to
            use words to get what you want...but crying is O.K.
            to let sadness out at any age.

Page 20.   WHEN PARENTS SEPARATE...Encourage children to think
            of a time when they felt very scared.
                    DRAW...SHARE

            (Drawing something frightening reduces a huge
            powerful picture in their mind to something small on
            a piece of paper. They feel empowered by being
            the drawer and in charge. They need to learn to
            share fears.

Page 21.   DIVORCE MAY ALSO BRING SOME GOOD CHANGES...
                    DRAW...SHARE

            (Children often draw that the fighting stops...
            or that a parent is happier...or that they get
            more time with one parent.) For some children
            it is difficult to see anything good.

MOVING ON: (DEFENSE MASKS) Have three masks showing the
            feelings of being happy, sad and angry. Pick
            two volunteers. Have one act one feeling wearing
            a mask...but keeping a different feeling inside.
            The other will respond to the actor.

            When finished, others may try. Ask them afterwards
            how it felt to be the actor...and how it felt to
            be the other person. (Masks or defensive feelings
            are like walls. They keep you from being close
            to the other person. It takes alot of energy to
            act differently than you feel.)

C. ENDING

    THIS WEEK: We talked about difficult feelings and learned
               O.K. ways to let feelings out.

    NEXT WEEK: We will talk about living with changes from divorce
               and learn how to take good care of ourselves.

    SCRIBBLE OUT:
               (SCRIBBLE OUT ANGER) Think about someone you
               often feel angry at. (This is often a sibling)
               Draw a symbol or stick person like that person
               with a red crayon. Think about your anger...
               put it on the paper by scribbling out

the symbol. Scribble really hard until the anger
is all gone. Next, scrunch the paper into a ball
and throw it at a blank wall. Finally throw it
in a waste basket and try to forget about it.
(Children love this. It is a healthy release
of anger. They may need to be reminded that this
doesn't hurt the person.)

UPS AND DOWNS:
What made you feel down today...and up today?

CREATIVE GOODBYE:
Thank them for sharing and working hard. Say
goodbye in the usual way.

SESSION V

LIVING WITH DIVORCED PARENTS p.22-27
Recognize parent's feelings
Increase confidence and self esteem
Learn ways to communicate concerns
Develop good self care

A. BEGINNING

SNACK: As before

GATHERING: Share a favorite memory...something they remember about
a time when they were happy and having fun.

SCRIBBLE IN:
On a sheet of newsprint, have children write the initials
of their first and last name. Add colors and lines to
turn the initials into a picture. They can turn the
paper any direction that works best.

CHECK IN: As group decided

B. CONTENT

LAST WEEK: We talked about difficult feelings and learned O.K.
ways to let them out.

TODAY: We will talk about living with changes from divorce and
learn how to take good care of ourselves.
(Read appropriate pages from book if desired.)

Page 22.   PARENTS HAVE MANY FEELINGS...Read
DRAW...SHARE

(Parents often feel differently about the divorce. They
may draw one smiling and the other sad or angry. Remind
children that people have different feelings at different
times. Feelings change. Children often want to fix
things for the sad parent. Remind them they can't fix
adult problems.)

Page 23.   PARENTS MAY NOT LIKE EACH OTHER...Read
DRAW...SHARE

(Children feel bad that the people they love are unkind
to each other. Unfortunately divorce doesn't end all
the fighting. Children gain their identity from both
parents and need to believe both are good people. They
can love the person and dislike the behavior.

Page 24.   EVERYONE HAS SOMETHING THEY WONDER OR WORRY ABOUT...Read
DRAW...SHARE

(Children need to know it is O.K. to ask questions, but
that not all questions can be answered. If addictions

have been involved, they have been living with rules of secrets and silence. They worry about causing more fighting. They also carry shame for things they don't dare ask about. They need courage to ask questions.

Page 25.   CHILDREN CAN SAY NO!   READ
                      DRAW...SHARE

(Children need to learn how to be safely assertive. If one parent has a drug or alcohol problem, it is helpful for them to attend a group for children of alcoholics where they will learn how to take care of themself.

Children can learn to refuse to listen to bad things about either parent. They often feel as if their heart is torn in half...and often shows in their drawing. Both parents often decide to work harder to resolve difficult issues.

Page 26.   CHILDREN NEED TO HELP... Read
                      DRAW...SHARE

(In single parent homes, more help is needed from the children. Appropriate chores and responsibilities are good. It builds self esteem and confidence. Yet, they should not be given responsibility beyond their years. They need time for friends and play and separation from parent's stress.

They need to know they can't replace a parent. They can't become a child escort to parties, a date or confident. Sharing the bed when frightened or lonely can become a problem.

Page 27.   THERE ARE THINGS I LIKE ABOUT ME...Read
                      DRAW...SHARE DURING THE MOVING ON

(Note children who draw just one thing or have a hard time thinking of anything. Help and encourage them to see what is good about them. Children are fearful about being unloveable and being abandoned by parents.

MOVING ON: (TALK AND TOSS) Hold a ball of yarn and explain rules. Only the person holding the yarn can talk. Toss the ball to a child and share one thing they like about themself...and then toss the ball across the group to someone else for their turn. Continue. A web will be be formed. Talk about relationships and connections.

Talk about the need for independence and inter-dependence.
Cut the yarn and give each child pieces to take home
to make a friendship bracelet...or this can be done
in group if there is time.

C. ENDING

THIS WEEK: We talked about ways we live happier with family changes.
You are learning to share feelings in this group and
you can do that with your parents also.

NEXT WEEK We will talk more about personal strengths and our
relationships with others. It will be our last week
for these groups and we will have a celebration.
(Some groups may decide to invite a parent to the
 celebration. If so plan accordingly.)

UPS AND DOWNS:
What do you feel down about...what do you feel good about?

SCRIBBLE OUT:
Play a peppy tape in the tape player you brought (opera
is good for a variety of feelings). Invite children
to use colors and lines to show what they hear in the
music. Begin with the dominant hand. After a few
minutes suggest they try the other hand. Compare.
(the dominant hand is usually less free)

CREATIVE GOODBYE:
Thank them and say goodbye as planned.

SESSION VI

LIVING WELL IN A CHANGING WORLD p.28-32
Recognize individual strengths
Identify support systems
Strengthen relationships
Celebrate book completion

A. BEGINNING

SNACK: Save snack for ending celebration. (cup cakes preferred)

GATHERING: (Before group begins, print these words on a piece of construction paper: PRETTY, HANDSOME, HONEST, STRONG, FRIENDLY, FUNNY, HELPFUL, CARING, NICE, NEAT, COOL, FOXY, GREAT.) Show sheet to children and ask them which 6 (or whatever the number in the group) they consider the most important. Give each child one of the chosen words to copy on colored slips of paper (about1"x2" the number in the group) and save for the moving on activity.

SCRIBBLE IN:

(ROAD MAP OF LIFE) On a sheet of newsprint, draw the ups and downs of your life so far...the road blocks, the bumpy times, the dead ends, the high times, the the bridges. Next, think ahead and draw a road map for your future. What good things do you hope for? Will there still be bumpy times?

CHECK IN: As decided by the group. Also ask how they feel about this being the last session.

B. CONTENT

LAST WEEK: We learned how to live well despite the changes in our family due to the divorce.

TODAY: We will look at ourselves and other important people in our world. (no time for pages from book usually)

Page 28. THERE ARE SOME THINGS I AM GOOD AT... Read. Encourage them to draw several things.
DRAW...SHARE

Page 29. THERE ARE SOME THINGS I LIKE TO DO WITH MOM...read. (This is more difficult for children than I expected. Let them begin on their own...but they may need some suggestions to pick from. They need to recognize it can be fun with one parent. Parents need help in knowing what they like to do with them.)
DRAW...SHARE

Page 30. THERE ARE THINGS I LIKE TO DO WITH DAD...read (same suggestions as above) Dads need to know they don't always have to do something special or spend money.

Page 31.   THERE WILL BE MANY GOOD TIMES. Read Invite them to
           list the people who are important to them. Next, place
           the number in the circle. This is a good time to
           explain relationships. Some people are close to you
           like parents and family. Others are not as close to
           you...you don't see them as often...but they are still
           important to you. Other grown ups in schools, churches
           and other places care alot about children also. (They
           need to know that many people care about them to feel
           more secure.)
                         DRAW...SHARE

           Ask them who they can talk to about problems. They
           can mark that person with a star.

           This is a good time to talk about relationships. Caring,
           sharing and working together makes good friendships.
           Talk about treating siblings with respect. Encourage
           them to practice group rules at home as well as in group.

Page 32.   I CAN WISH FOR SOME HAPPY CHANGES....Read.
                         DRAW...SHARE

           (They may wish for their parents to get back together
           again. They can be told this seldom happens but
           they can wish for parents to both be happy. They may
           or may not wish their parent will marry someone else.
           They need to accept the permanence of divore. They
           may wish for a happy marriage and family of their own
           when they grow up. They fear making similar mistakes.)

           Mainly, they need to know there will be more changes in
           their life as they grow up, but they have learned good
           coping skills and they will be O.K.

MOVING ON: (POSITIVE OBSTACLES) Arrange chairs for a simple
           obstacle course to crawl under or climb over. Give
           children a spot to stand and the positive statement
           slips they made earlier in this session. Take turns
           going around the course, stopping to recieve a slip
           from each child as they say, "You are...or are going
           to be (which ever they choose to say)_____.
           The facilitator takes the place of the child going
           around and hands out their slip while they are gone.
           The children keep their slips to paste on a sheet with
           the group photo.

CELEBRATION:
           Take a group picture using a polaroid camera (or a
           regular camera the week before and get prints) Have
           an 8x10 sheet of colored construction paper for the
           children to glue the picture and the positive words on.
           Let each child sign their name to the sheet so they
           will have something to remember their time together.

C. ENDING

THIS WEEK: We have had our 6th and last session. You have worked really hard and I have enjoyed our time together. I feel good about the things you have learned.

SCRIBBLE OUT:

(GROUP MURAL) Before the session begins, draw the grief "wave" from page 8 in the workbook with a black marker on a white piece of butcher paper about 10 ft. long. Tape to a wall. Invite children to decorate the mural with different feelings of grief in appropriate places and appropriate colors and pictures. Decorate as they wish. Suggest they finish by writing O.K. in empty spaces to remind them that all feelings are O.K.

Ask children for permission to keep the mural as a memory of the group and something you might be able to use to teach others about children's grief.

UPS AND DOWNS:

As usual, but allow time for them to express feelings about the group ending. Some may have some sadness or anger. They may choose to have a reunion some time.

CREATIVE GOODBYE:

Suggest a final review of what they have learned together:
Change is a natural part of life.
Divorce creates change and losses.
Loss creates many feelings of grief.
Parents may divorce each other but not their children.
Feelings need to be expressed in healthy ways.
You are important and many people care about you.

Tell them their book will be a reminder of their time here and the things they learned. Encourage them to share the book with their parents because they can learn from it too.

Thank them for being part of the group and for the things you have learned from them. Wish them well and ask them if they would like to say goodbye in a special way. (a group hug is great if they want to. This is another ending for them.)

Bibliography

ART THERAPY

COCUZZA/ZAMBELLI. "USE OF ART WITH CHILDREN IN THE BEREAVEMENT PROCESS", PROCEEDINGS OF THE AATA CONF. 1982, AATA PUB.

DALLEY, TESSA, "ART AS THERAPY" London: Tavistock Pub. 1984

FURTH, GREG. "THE SECRET WORLD OF DRAWINGS". Boston: Sigo Press, 1988

GARDNER, HOWARD. "ARTFUL SCRIBBLES." N.Y.: Basic BOoks, 1980

KRAMER, EDITH, "ART AS THERAPY WITH CHILDREN". N.Y.: SCHOCKEN BOOKS, 1971

LANDGARTEN, HELEN B., "CLINICAL ART THERAPY". N.Y.: BRUNNER/MAZEL PUB., 1981

MUSANTE, J. L. "AN EXPLORATION OF GRIEF AND ART THERAPY". PROCEEDINGS OF AT CONF. 1976, AATA PUB. 1981-83

OAKLANDER, VIOLET. "WINDOWS TO OUR CHILDREN". Moab, Utah: Real People Press, 1978

OSTER, GERALD & GOULD, PATRICIA. "USING DRAWING IN ASSESSMENT AND THERAPY." N.Y.: Brunner/Mazel 1978

RUBIN, JUDITH. "CHILD ART THERAPY". N.Y.: Van Nostrand Reinhold Co. 1978

SIMON, RITA. "BEREAVEMENT ART". AMERICAN JOURNAL OF ART THERAPY, VOL. 20, JULY 1981

CHILDREN

BRIGGS, DOROTHY. "YOUR CHILD'S SELF-ESTEEM". Garden City, NY Doubleday & Co. 1970

CLARK, JEAN. "SELF-ESTEEM: A FAMILY AFFAIR". MINNEAPOLIS: WINSTON PRESS, 1978

DREIKURS, RUDOLF. "CHILDREN: THE CHALLENGE." N.Y.: Hawthorne BOoks, 1964

ERICKSON, ERICK. "IDENTITY: YOUTH & CRISIS". N.Y.: NORTON, 1968

FONTENELL, D. "UNDERSTANDING AND MANAGING OVER ACTIVE CHILDREN". ENGLEWOOD CLIFFS, N.J.: PRENTICE HALL, 1983

KERSEY, KATHERINE. "HELPING YOUR CHILD HANDLE STRESS". WASH. D.C.: ACROPOLIS BOOK LTD, 1986

LEVIN, PAMELA. "BECOMING THE WAY WE ARE". Winatchee, Wa.: Directed Media Inc. 1974

PIAGET, J. "THE PSYCHOLOGY OF THE CHILD". N.Y.: BASIC BOOKS, 1969

SHELLEY, JUDITH. "THE SPIRITUAL NEEDS OF CHILDREN". DOWNERS GROVE, IL: INTERVARSITY PRESS, 1982

SEPARATION AND LOSS

BOWLBY, JOHN. "LOSS: SADNESS & DEPRESSION". N.Y.: BASIC BOOKS, 1980

FURMAN, E. "A CHILD'S PARENT DIES". N.Y.: YALE UNIV. PRESS, 1974

FURMAN, ROBT. A. "THE PSYCHOANALYTIC STUDY OF THE CHILD". N.Y.: INTERNATIONAL UNIVERSITIES PRESS, 1964

GORDON/KLASS. "THEY NEED TO KNOW". N.J.: PRENTICE HALL, 1979

GROLLMAN, EARL A. "EXPLAINING DEATH TO CHILDREN". BOSTON: BEACON PRESS, 1970

JACKSON, EDGAR N. "TELLING A CHILD ABOUT DEATH". N.Y.: HAWTHORN/DULTON, 1965

JEWETT, CLAUDIA. "HELPING CHILDREN COPE WITH SEPARATION AND LOSS". LONDON: TRAVISTOCK PUB., 1984

KLEIN, KENNETH M. "TOPICS IN PEDIATRICS/SPRING 1982". MINNEAPOLIS CHILDREN'S HEALTH CENTER PUB.

KREMETZ, JILL. "HOW IT FEELS WHEN A PARENT DIES". N.Y.: KNOPF, 1981

KRUPNICK, JANICE L. "BEREAVEMENT DURING CHILDHOOD AND ADOLESCENCE" IN BERAVEMENT; REACTION, CONSEQUENCES AND CARE. OSTERWEIS, M. et all NATIONAL ACADEMY PRESS, 1984

KUENING, DELORES. "HELPING PEOPLE THROUGH GRIEF" MPLS. BETHANY HOUSE, 1987

KUBLER-Ross, ELIZABETH. "ON CHILDREN AND DEATH". N.Y.: Macmillan Pub. 1983

MILLS/REISLER, ROBINSON/VERMILZE. "DISCUSSING DEATH: A GUIDE TO DEATH EDUCATION". E.T.C. PUB., 1976

O'TOOLE, DONNA. "GROWING THROUGH GRIEF". Mount Rainbow Pub., Burnsville, NC 1989

STRICKLAND., ALBERT AND LYNNE DeSPELDER, "THE LAST DANCE: ENCOUNTERING DEATH & DYING". PALO ALTO, CA.: MAYFIELD PUB., 1983

THOMAS, JAMES L. "DEATH AND DYING IN THE CLASSROOM", READINGS FOR REFERENCE. ORYX PRESS. 1984

WASS, H & CORR, C. "CHILDHOOD AND DEATH". WASH. D.C.: HEMISPHERE PUB.,

WORDEN, J. "PERSONAL DEATH AWARENESS". ENGLEWOOD CLIFFS, N.J.: PRENTICE HALL, INC., 1976

WORDEN, WILLIAM J. "GRIEF COUNSELING AND GRIEF THERAPY: A HANDBOOK FOR THE MENTAL HEALTH PRACTIONER, N.Y. SPRINGER CO.. 1982

WOLFELT, A. "HELPING CHILDREN COPE WITH GRIEF." Muncie, Ind.: Accelerated Development, Inc. 1983

The Drawing Out Feelings Series

Woodland Press

This new series designed by Marge Heegaard provides parents and professionals with an organized approach to helping children ages 6-12 cope with feelings resulting from family loss and change.

Designed to be used in an adult/child setting, these workbooks provide age-appropriate educational concepts and questions to help children identify and accept their feelings. Children are given the opportunity to work out their emotions during difficult times while learning to recognize acceptable behavior, and conflicts can be resolved and self-esteem increased while the coping skills for loss and change are being developed.

All four titles are formatted so that children can easily illustrate their answers to the important questions in the text.

When Someone Very Special Dies

Children Can Learn To Cope With Grief
MARGE HEEGAARD

A workbook to help children work out feelings about death.

36 pp., 11" x 8 1/2"
$6.95, paperback
ISBN 0-9620502-0-2

Heegaard provides a practical format for allowing children to understand the concepts of death and develop coping skills for life. Children, with the supervision of an adult, are invited to illustrate and personalize their loss through art. *When Someone Very Special Dies* encourages the child to identify support systems and personal strengths.

"I especially appreciate the design of this book...the child becomes an active participant in pictorially and verbally doing something about their loss." Dean J. Hempel, M.D.
Child Psychiatrist

When Someone Has A Very Serious Illness

Children Can Learn To Cope With Loss and Change
MARGE HEEGAARD

A workbook to help children deal with feelings about serious illness.

When someone has a serious illness, everyone in the family is affected. While the family focus is on a long-term illness, children may develop unhealthy defenses and roles. *When Someone Has A Very Serious Illness* invites children to illustrate the text and encourages them to talk about their misconceptions, fears and worries. In addition, they also learn about basic concepts of illness and healthier ways of coping with someone's illness.

41 pp., 11" x 8 1/2"
$6.95, paperback
ISBN 0-9620502-4-5

"This is an important book. When serious illness comes into a family, all members...including children...must deal with change. This book offers a positive tool for coping with those many changes." Christine Ternand, M.D.
Pediatric Endocrinologist

When Something Terrible Happens

Children Can Learn To Cope With Grief
MARGE HEEGAARD

A workbook to help children work out feelings about a traumatic event.

Acts of violence by man or nature and other terrible things can and do happen in a child's world. Traumatic events in the lives of their families, friends or community leave children feeling confused, insecure and frightened. Recreating an overwhelming event on paper reduces the child's terror and creates feelings of empowerment. Drawing puts the child in charge and provides the opportunity for the exploration of feelings related to helplessness and fear. With the help of *When Something Terrible Happens*, nightmares and post-traumatic stress symptoms can be relieved.

36 pp., 11" x 8 1/2"
$6.95, paperback
ISBN 0-9620502-3-7

"This healing book...combines story, pictures, information and art therapy in a way that appeals to children." Stephanie Frogge,
Director of Victim
Outreach, M.A.D.D.

When Mom and Dad Separate

Children Can Learn To Cope With
Grief from Divorce
MARGE HEEGAARD

A workbook to help children work out their feelings about separation and divorce.

Divorce creates stressful feelings of grief from loss and change, and children who are unable to understand or verbally express their feelings often act them out in unhealthy ways. *When Mom and Dad Separate* discusses basic concepts of marriage and divorce and offers young minds a creative way to sort out and express all the powerful feelings resulting from their parents' decision to separate.

36 pp., 11" x 8 1/2"
$6.95, paperback
ISBN 0-9620502-2-9

"A wonderfully wise book that will inform, prepare, guide, encourage and support both children and parents through the pain of divorce. Most importantly, it not only offers understanding, but hope."
Rabbi Dr. Earl A. Grollman

Facilitator Guide For
DRAWING OUT FEELINGS

NEW...FACILITATOR GUIDE
for
When Someone Very Special Dies
When Something Terrible Happens
When Someone Has a Very Serious Illness
When Mom and Dad Separate

Structure and suggestions for helping children, individually or in groups, cope with feelings from family change. Includes directions for six organized sessions for each of the four workbooks.
114 pp. 8½x11 ISBN 0-9620502-5-3
$20.00

36 pp., 11" x 8 1/2"
$6.95, paperback
ISBN 0-9620502-6-1

WHEN A PARENT MARRIES AGAIN
CHILDREN CAN LEARN TO COPE WITH FAMILY CHANGE
written by Marge Heegaard to be illustrated by children

"This interactive children's volume is a must read for children 6-12 who may live or are living in a stepfamily. Adults too will appreciate and learn from this book."
Judith L. Bauersfeld, Ph.D.
President
STEPFAMILY ASSOC. OF AMERICA

About The Author

Marge Heegaard, MA, ATR, LICSW, is a Registered Art Therapist and a Certified Grief Counselor in private practice in Minneapolis. She has been a leader in developing grief support for children using the art process to express feelings of loss and change. In addition to the *Drawing Out Feelings* series, Marge Heegaard is the author of *Coping With Death and Grief* and co-author of *When a Family Gets Diabetes*. Her books are enjoyed and recommended by parents, educators, counselors, social workers, clergy, physicians and other professionals.

Grades 3-6
64 pages *$15.95*

Stories about young people's grief and facts about death.

Coping with
Death & Grief